GHOSTS:

On the Square . . .

And Elsewhere. . . .

Ghosts: On the Square . . . And Elsewhere. . . .

Published by Southern Indiana Writers, 2200 Reno Ave., New Albany, IN, 47150
Book designed by T. Lee Harris

ISBN 978-0-615-25202-5

Cover design and photo-manipulation by T. Lee Harris

Cover Photo by Marian Allen

Ghosts:
On the Square . . .

And Elsewhere....

Photos, photo manipulations and illustrations:

Marian Allen 8,39, 52, 69, 111

Joanna Foreman 14

Ginny Fleming 31, 87, 93

T. Lee Harris 36, 43, 51, 57, 73, 83, 91

Eric Jaremczuk 100

Joy Kirchgessner 5, 21, 27, 33, 45

Ardis Moonlight 25

Teddi Robinson 6-7 & 58-59

GHOSTS:

On the Square . . .

Carnegie Library

The Pink Mystery

by

Joanna Foreman

On the evening of March 31, 1987, the flight attendant made the day's final announcement: "Ladies and gentlemen, welcome to Louisville. Due to the ongoing strike, you may experience a significant delay at Baggage Claim. We appreciate your patience during this difficult labor issue and apologize for any inconvenience. Once again, thank you for flying Delta."

I stepped off the jet way and headed for a lounge to kill time. I came close to ordering a cold brew but decided I'd had more than enough alcohol during my wild spring break in Key West. A fresh cup of coffee would better suit me; there'd be tons of unpacking to do when I got home to Corydon.

As I savored the java, I noticed an outrageous headline through the glass window of a newspaper box:

ORANGE GLOWING SPACESHIPS COMMONPLACE IN
CORYDON!

The front-page article was short with sketchy details and, wouldn't you know, I was fresh out of coins. I was eager to see what all the excitement was about, but when I got home the front porch was devoid of a pile of week-old newspapers. Probably Grandma's doing. She wouldn't have wanted it to appear obvious that I was gone—you know—attracting burglars and the like. I considered calling her, but she goes to bed early and doesn't take kindly to being awakened. I yawned, reconciling myself to the fact that I was out of luck for the night.

Early the next morning, I threw a load of clothes into the washer and walked a few blocks along Chestnut to the library at Oak and Beaver Streets. A gray-haired librarian, wearing a long, paisley dress, stood next to a cart of returned paperbacks. On her collar was pinned a large button that read *Octogenarian*. Leave it to a librarian to accessorize with a six-syllable word. She directed me to the appropriate department, where I gathered up the last two weeks' worth of newspapers. I seated

myself at a large desk and pored through various articles. The news carried a recurring theme: a good number of verified sightings of strange nocturnal lights near Corydon had been reported during March. The credibility of the witnesses could not be questioned because they were all intelligent and responsible citizens of Harrison County. The idea of UFOs as a hoax was not a consideration at all . . . and here *I'd* gone off and missed the entire phenomenon.

Suddenly, I felt, more than heard, a whisper and sensed I was being watched. I looked all around but could see no one except the ancient-and-proud-of-it-librarian, busier than ever at the front counter. I shook off the creepy feeling, closed my eyes and leaned back in my chair. What would it have been like to see a genuine flying saucer? I'd have loved to witness those glowing orange lights in the sky—something to tell my grandchildren about someday. If only I had been in Harrison County instead of traipsing around Key West bars at night; lounging on beaches in the afternoons; and watching con artists' performances on Mallory Square against backdrops of jewel-toned sunsets. Late one night, after celebrating my twenty-first birthday with a margarita the size of a fish tank, my friends had dared me to visit Madam Bellina on Duvall Street, a psychic with an honest-to-goodness crystal ball. I recalled her Gypsy-like appearance: ankle-length black skirt, white peasant blouse and, thrown over her shoulders, was a black shawl with hundreds of little silver coins and beads dangling from its edges. She wore a heap of neck chains, rings on every finger and a jingling ankle bracelet. Her make-up—parrot-green eye shadow and black lipstick—was so entirely gaudy that I couldn't take her seriously. As she read my tarot cards, she raised one eyebrow and her face turned to chalk. It was well worth the twenty-five dollars I'd paid, and I wondered if she put on that type of show for everyone who walked through her door.

The memory caused me to laugh out loud, but then I remembered I was in a library, and I quickly opened my eyes to see if I had disturbed anyone. What I saw caused me to nearly fall off my chair.

A pale pink swatch of thin, gauze fabric floated past me, right in front of my face, and disappeared into thin air! I definitely heard the whisper again . . . *The librarian knows. . . .*

What the librarian knew was a mystery to me. Call it jet lag, vacation let-down, or just an over-active imagination, one thing was for sure—the goose bumps on my arms and the shivers that went through me from top to bottom were real enough. Maybe it was low blood sugar; I hadn't eaten anything today. Whatever. I'd learned all I wanted to know about the UFOs. I selected Ann Tyler's latest novel and checked out.

I hurried home to a pot of hot tea, sausage links and scrambled eggs, and reached into my book bag for something to take my mind off the weird library occurrence. I found not one, but *two* books in there, the second one being a yellowed, hardbound historical account of great Ohio River floods. I examined the volume and speculated how it had gotten into my canvas bag. The book was stamped on the inside cover *REFERENCE DEPARTMENT.* It should not have been removed from the library at all! Oh great, I thought; now I'd have to sneak it back in past the librarian who knew . . . what?

I transferred my laundry from the washer to the dryer, cleaned the breakfast dishes and walked, once again, over to Beaver Street. Hoping to make myself invisible, I calmly sauntered past the syllable queen as though I didn't have a care in the world.

"Forget something, dear?" she inquired, squinting above her narrow reading glasses.

"Oh, uh," I muttered. "I think I may have left my pink neck scarf. Have you by any chance seen it?"

"*Pink*, you say? Oh dear," she murmured. "Hmm, no . . . not a neck scarf that I recall . . . umm. . . . I"ll keep my eyes open."

"You do that, if you can," I mumbled quietly to myself. Her stare bored a hole through me as I walked to the back of the library. Had she seen something *else* pink, as I had?

In the Reference Department I found a spot for the book. Its official title was *Unsolved Mysteries of the Ohio River Floods.* I located the catalog number and tucked it firmly into the shelf, right where it belonged.

After shuffling the few blocks back to my house, I kicked off my sneakers, started another load of laundry and lit a fire in the fireplace. I nuked a mug of hot cocoa and curled up on my sofa with Grandma's afghan.

I'd made my way through the first three chapters of *The Accidental Tourist* when I got up to stoke the fire.

Unsolved Mysteries of the Ohio River Floods lay on my coffee table!

What in the world? Madame Bellina had warned me that something unusual would happen, but don't all psychics tell you that? I had snickered when she predicted it, and at this moment I was feeling just a tiny bit of regret for doing so.

I reached for the old book and thumbed through, reading a few pages here and there, and set it back down on the table. I hadn't realized there were any mysteries associated with the Ohio River floods, but apparently some folks had gone missing and were never found. The floods were blamed, at first, but a prominent theory was later proposed that some had disappeared on purpose, finding the flood a good excuse as any. What a great scheme, if it worked, I thought, but surely some of those bodies had eventually shown up somewhere along the line, probably unidentifiable.

I needed a comforting voice, so I called Grandma to let her know I'd made it home from Florida.

"Did you hear about our UFOs? Oh, you missed it, Honey," she said excitedly. "Walk your pretty little self on down here for lunch, you hear? I'll tell you all about it."

My grandma eats a hearty breakfast at five o'clock in the morning, lunch at two in the afternoon and is in bed by six. She claims that's how she's lived so long. She's sixty-eight now, which really isn't old at all. I'd walk over to see her around two.

I re-stoked the fire, pulled the afghan up closer and settled back into my novel. Before long, I drifted off to sleep. I dreamed of a girl, all dressed up in pink: a street-length cotton dress, gloves and a matching ribbon tied into her long blonde hair. Her feet were adorned with sparkling pink ballet slippers. She was dancing around the room, singing. Suddenly, she handed me a book, pointing to a specific page.

I awakened with a start. The house was unusually quiet, with only the occasional hiss and sputter of a glowing orange log.

I glanced at the coffee table but the library book was no longer there! Had this all been a dream? But, wait. My Ann Tyler novel was on the coffee table, and the Ohio River mysteries book was in my lap!

How could *that* be? I was not a known sleepwalker, yet the only logical explanation I could come up with was that I had somehow exchanged the two books during my nap. A strip of faded pink gauze, tied in knots, marked the place of a story entitled "Can Pinkie Find her Way Home?"

Madam Bellina's words echoed in my ears: *YOU WILL HELP A LITTLE GIRL FIND HER WAY HOME!*

> Jane (a.k.a. Pinkie) Poppersham, a charming sliver of a girl, went missing the very same day the river overtook much of Corydon's square. It is rumored she was last seen in the library. A fifth-grader and an avid reader, Pinkie could be found there most afternoons after school, doing homework or reading her favorite mystery stories. On that fateful day, Pinkie's mother became aware of the approaching danger of floodwater and ran to the library. As she rushed through the front door and into the vestibule, she noted that the basement was entirely flooded, and brown, mucky water was spilling onto the first floor. The librarian insisted Pinkie had not entered the library that day. The two women worked together getting other patrons to safety, after which time several neighbors joined Pinkie's mother in a search for her daughter until well after dusk, but to no avail.

Poppersham—such an unusual name. I thought I'd seen it before, somewhere. I read a little more of the story, as I was curious where her nickname, Pinkie, had come from. Ever since she was a toddler, the child had preferred the color pink, and by the age of seven she refused to wear clothing of any other color! Neighbors insisted they had seen the girl enter the library earlier that day. Although her body was never found, Pinkie Poppersham was listed as a casualty of the flood. Foul play had not been suspected.

My major in college is English. The least of my interests is history, and in high school I had truly suffered through those required classes, World History and American History. I couldn't abide the study of Ohio River floods, some of which having occurred over fifty years ago. Why would I ever want to know about that? Now, I had to admit

the stories were interesting, even though I was annoyed that the old book seemed to have a mind of its own, inconveniencing me to no end. I tossed it onto the coffee table and folded my clean clothes.

It was nearly two o'clock. I had borrowed Grandma's set of red crocodile luggage for my trip. I'd return it and see what she thought of the entire scenario. If anyone could remember this Pinkie situation, it would be Grandma.

In Grandma's kitchen, I opened her overnight case and removed the library book, along with a souvenir—a silver-plated collector's spoon with an enamel design on the handle in the shape of Florida. She kissed me on the forehead and placed the spoon in a wooden display rack on the wall next to her antique Hoosier cupboard.

She flipped up the leaves of her oak kitchen table, and we lunched on Campbell's tomato soup, triangle-shaped tuna salad sandwiches on whole-wheat toast, deviled eggs and peach pie. Grandma went on about the unusual sightings in Corydon skies. She knew everyone in Harrison County, so naturally she knew the handful of people who had seen UFOs in their backyards. She said she even saw an orange glow herself. I thought that might be a stretch, but who am I to question her? I listened patiently until she had finished her reporting duties. She seemed happy that I had been away, thus leaving someone she could share the gossip with. Everyone else around here had gotten it firsthand or from the daily news broadcasts.

She stared at me like she was seeing me for the first time. "You needn't be so frightened . . . and pale, Honey. The lights have been gone now for nearly two weeks. I doubt they'll come back," Grandma soothed.

I took a deep breath. "It's not aliens I'm afraid of, Grandma. It's this book," I said as I shoved it across the table. "And the color pink, and the library, and . . . oh dear . . . I'm not making sense at all, am I?"

She looked at the library book and her brow wrinkled. She covered my hand with hers, giving it a few pats. "Start from the very beginning," Grandma said softly.

So I did. I told her about the Gypsy fortune teller, the library, the book and my dream. Grandma was on the edge of her seat and the more I talked the more serious the look on her face, until *she* became

somewhat pale herself.

"Okay, now," I demanded. "What is it that everyone else seems to know but me?"

"Why, it's your house. *You* bought the Poppersham house. Check the deed—it's on there. Of course, it's had several owners since the flood. But the house is yours now, I'm afraid."

So *that's* where I'd seen the name—on my deed. "Do you mean my house is haunted?"

"No, I don't believe it's the house per se. I think it may be the library, though."

"The library . . . I don't understand."

"Think about it. Where did you first get a glimpse of that pink gauze?"

"Well . . . the library," I said.

"And the book followed you home, right?"

"Twice."

"Exactly! That must mean that Pinkie really *did* drown in the library, and she has chosen *you* to help her come home, to her family and a suitable grave." She scooted back comfortably into her chair, pursed her lips, and folded her hands matter-of-factly, just the same way she does when she wins at Bingo.

"But . . ," I argued. "Exactly where is her body? It was never found, you know. If she wants a proper burial she'd better be leading me to her body, I'd say."

That night I went to bed wearing my jeans and a long-sleeved sweatshirt. I placed my sneakers on the floor so I could easily slip them on. I knew what would happen next, and I wanted to be prepared.

Around two o'clock in the morning, I awakened to find her standing at the foot of my bed. I wasn't the least bit frightened because Grandma had assured me that Pinkie was one of the sweetest little girls she'd ever known. Grandma was seven years older but they'd lived in the same neighborhood and played together often. Grandma had been her babysitter for a few years and confided she'd been devastated when Pinkie disappeared. She warned me of only one thing: "Whatever happens, don't tell your worry-wart mother about any of this. She's paranoid enough about her only daughter living alone."

I stared at Pinkie in the moonlit bedroom for a minute or so. I saw that she had been a beautiful child. She was wearing the same pink dress she'd died in, I supposed, only it was in shreds . . . shreds of pale, pink gauze. She had a silk, pink ribbon in her hair, and she wore pink ballet slippers.

She reached for me and I held my hand out to her. I slipped out of bed and into my shoes. She led me out the front door and up to the library. Along the way she tried to explain how she died and why she ended up missing, but her voice gradually diminished, and I couldn't get a grasp of everything she said. We crept alongside the building toward the back to the massive pine tree. It stood quiet and elegant, with a full moon casting colossal pine shadows all the way across Chestnut Street. Pinkie motioned for me to sit down on a crescent-shaped concrete bench, and she lowered herself to the ground and leaned against the vast trunk.

"Is this it, Pinkie? Is this where we can find your body?"

"The librarian knows . . ." Pinkie whispered. Then she disappeared. Not in a fast way, but slow like . . . she just simply faded away.

I sat there for a while longer, figuring out what to do next. I took Grandma's wise advice about not letting my mother in on this secret. When I finally came up with a plan, and I was satisfied it would work, I went back home and slept better than I've slept for a long time. Until five o'clock, when my phone rang. Of course it was Grandma.

"Well?"

"Oh, golly gee. Good morning, Grandma. You woke me up. Can I call you back later?"

"No, you certainly may not. I want to know what's happening to my favorite granddaughter."

"I'm your *only* granddaughter."

"That's beside the point. Now get on with it."

So I told her the story of Pinkie's visit and our little outing under the evergreen tree. I explained what I planned to do about it.

"Good idea. Now we wait," she said. "Go back to sleep." She hung up.

The next afternoon I was out for a walk and saw a small group

congregated around the big, old evergreen tree. The librarian was one of them, and she appeared to be crying. I tried my best not to stare. My plan had worked—so far. A couple of days later it was all over the news. The librarian claimed she had found what appeared to be a human bone while planting flowers beside the tree trunk. Her story didn't sound at all like the one Pinkie had told me, but it got the job done. The police dug around and found Pinkie's remains, and the following week the Poppersham family buried them in an oak coffin lined with pink taffeta in their family plot. I skipped class and accompanied Grandma to the graveside service.

The memorial was to be at one o'clock, and by noon a good-sized crowd had developed at the gravesite. Behind me someone tapped my shoulder. I turned around and what did I find but my mother's scowling face smack-dab in front of mine.

"What on earth are *you* doing here?" she demanded. "Don't you have class today?"

Grandma nudged my knee with hers, and she spoke up. "I asked her to bring me. You know how fond I was of Pinkie, and I didn't want *you* to miss work."

My mother chewed on the inside of her lip and glanced back at me. "Humph. I'm here now. I'll take over with Grandma. You run along to your classes."

Right about then, in the far distant section of the cemetery, a flash of pink caught my eye, and I said, "Good idea, Mom."

Grandma was shocked, because she knew how desperately I had wanted to attend Pinkie's funeral.

I grasped her hand. "Come with me and get your jacket before I leave," I said. "And, Mom, save her place . . . she'll be right back."

We hurried to my car and checked to see if my mother was watching. Thank goodness she was deep in conversation with a neighbor. We collected Grandma's jacket, hopped across a narrow driveway and stood behind a large tombstone. In no time, Pinkie appeared. Dressed in an elegant, soft pink dress, she looked very much at peace.

She extended her hand toward Grandma and said, "It's heavenly to see you again, Maggie."

Grandma was all tears and seemed to have lost her voice. "What really happened to you, Pinkie?" she said, finally, her voice shaking.

"You remember Buddy, the librarian's little brother who cleaned the library bathrooms?"

Grandma nodded as she grasped the tissue I had handed her.

"Well, the day of the flood, he was messing around in the basement. He shouldn't have been down there in the first place, but I saw him go down, and so did the librarian. She didn't say anything, an expert, even then, at keeping her mouth shut. Anyway, when the water came pouring in, she stood there, frozen. I figured she couldn't swim, so I bolted down the stairs and into the water to get him. He bobbed up and down and screamed, so I got over to him and grabbed him, but he struggled—panicked I guess—and pushed me away. The water pressure slammed my head against one of those old columns. Buddy somehow got to the surface and just stood there halfway up the stairs and watched me cry out over and over for help. Then, when I went under for the last time, he told his sister what he'd done. That night they dug a hole by the big tree in the back yard and slid my body into it. I hovered— watched the whole thing—it was freaky, let me tell you." Pinkie shuddered. "Buddy was slow, you remember, Maggie?"

Grandma nodded energetically. "Slightly retarded."

"And he talked kinda funny, too, you know?" Pinkie said. "Why, I was one of the few kids in school who *never* made fun of him, and then he treated me that-a-way. Sheesh!"

Pinkie raised one eyebrow and winked. "I've been haunting them both ever since."

Grandma and I looked at one another in amazement.

"Buddy figured out just last year that, if he stayed far enough away from the library, I couldn't reach him. But the old gal, well, she just doesn't get it, I guess. I don't know, maybe she tolerates it as part of her punishment, or something." Pinkie frowned. "But the thrill, for me, is long gone now."

"But, what are you going to do about the librarian?" I asked. "She hasn't admitted anything at all!"

"No, but so what? She's paid dearly through the years, trust me." Pinkie giggled, and then regained her composure. "Besides, what good would it do my family to know the truth? This way they think I

was a flood victim overtaken by Ohio River sediment. I got what I wanted. I'm ready to go home, and I can, thanks to you." She turned to face Grandma. "Did you know your granddaughter put a note on that old biddy's front door? Told her she'd better come clean—or else. She signed it Jane Poppersham—in *PINK*." She looked over at me. "A brilliant touch, by the way." She handed me a tiny, gold locket. "My dear mother put this in my coffin, but I'll have no use for it, really. I'd like you to have it."

Pinkie pointed toward the crowd of people gathered across the lawn. "I'd better get over there. Looks like they're about ready to start saying wonderful things about me, and I don't want to miss *that*," she said, smiling, "and . . . *I* have a *soul-train* to catch!"

Posey House

The Sensitive
by
Ardis Moonlight

They buried Poppa a year ago. After the funeral, the doctor and Faith, our housekeeper, helped Mother up the stairs to her bedroom. She hasn't been down since.

The only time I see Mother is in the morning. Faith has told me she isn't good to be around in the afternoon or evening. "Her temper isn't pleasant, and she cries so much. I'm worried about her. Even the doctor doesn't know what to do."

I have dreaded the visits, not about seeing Mother, but what's happening to her room. Just a few weeks after she started staying up-stairs, I noticed tears running down the deep blue wallpaper in her bedroom. Water was pooling on the floor. Seeing Poppa's ghost near the doorway helped—he would smile at me. Of course, I didn't tell Mother about seeing ghosts—I did once.

In the afternoons for an hour, I practice my piano lessons in the parlor. It has dark red wallpaper and a large painted portrait of a man. It's the best time for me because Mother's asleep from the medication Faith gives her. I can lose myself in music; however, I couldn't help noticing the man sitting under the portrait. He started appearing a month after Poppa's death. He was always sipping something in a glass. One day, I realized he was the man in the portrait. He looked somewhat like Poppa.

This morning's visit was horrible. When I knocked on the door, Mother's weak voice creaked, "Come in, Charity."

As always, she lay like a faded white rose in the four-poster bed, and the man from the parlor sat in the chair near the window, murmuring, "Hettie. My Hettie."

Poppa leaned near the doorway. Today, the water was knee deep, and drops pounced on the surface. I glanced up. There were tears on the ceiling, too. I waded slowly through the cold, dark water to the bed, my dress bunching around my ankles.

"Charity!" Mother moved her right arm and clasped my hand.

Hers was so thin, yet still so strong.

"Good morning, Momma. How are you feeling?"

"Tired. How are you?"

"I'm well. I miss you so much."

Mother's still-thick lips barely smiled.

"Momma, come downstairs today and listen to me play. I've gotten very good on the Beethoven piece."

"Not today, Charity."

It was always the same conversation. I wished I could carry her outside, show her the horses and cows, and walk with her to Indian Creek. I looked at Poppa, who smiled. I was desperate.

"Momma, Poppa said you need to get up and start living again. He wants to leave, but he can't until you let him go!"

Out of the corner of my eye, I could see Poppa nodding.

Mother's eyes widened, then narrowed. Her face went from too white to almost black. She ballooned in size; anger flooded the room. Her hand tightened then she shoved me away. Waves crashed against the walls and knocked me underwater.

Mother screamed, each word biting my ears, "ARE YOU SEE-ING GHOSTS AGAIN, CHARITY? YOU HAVE A PACT WITH THE DEVIL? GET OUT! GET OUT!

If Poppa hadn't pulled me, I believe I would have drowned. The door slammed. I stood in the hall, gasping.

Faith rushed up the stairs. "What happened?"

"I upset Momma. Now she hates me!" I cried. Faith pulled me against her short, plump body, and murmured, "Lettie Douglass just doesn't want to let go."

The biscuits with strawberry jam and milk tasted good. I nibbled another one of Faith's renowned biscuits, feeling much better sitting in the kitchen with her. "What is wrong with Momma?"

Faith was quiet. She looked at me. "She's doing what some people call wallowing in misery. She's lost interest in living."

"But I'm here."

"I know, child." She patted me, her touch so different from Mother's. "It's hard, seeing your mother like this. She reminds me of someone I once knew."

"Who?"

"You know the portrait in the parlor?" I nodded, my mouth full of biscuit.

"That's Colonel Tom Posey. He built this house more than 50 years ago. He and Aunt Hettie—she was a former slave of his father's—lived here about 30 or more years. Together they raised 14 orphans. When she died right after Christmas the first year of the War, he grieved something awful. He would sit in the parlor and drink every night, drink himself to sleep. After a few months, he was too lonely, so he upped and went to visit his nephew in Henderson, miles down the river over in Kentucky, and never came back. He died about two years after Hettie. He's buried there."

"Aunt Hettie was a slave?"

"Yes, but he freed her. Your mother reminds me of her in a way."

"She's not a Negro!"

"Well, Hettie wasn't much of one, either. She was part that and part white—kind of golden color. She was beautiful and intelligent. She even wrote poetry—I liked to hear her read."

"You knew them?"

"Yes, I was one of the orphans."

I could barely sleep, trying to figure a way to get Mother to want to live again. Maybe if I told her the story of Colonel Posey and Hettie she would find it as interesting as I did. The soft rain made me sleepy.

I awoke. The rain was pouring on the roof, Mother was sobbing, thunder shook the bed, and wind clawed the house. Then I heard the urgency in a deep voice outside crying, "Hettie! Where are you, Hettie?"

I was surprised at the water sloshing against my bed and the curtains billowing against the window with rain spraying in. I had to move quickly. I jumped into the water, wading as fast as I could to the window in a wet nightgown. When I leaned out, I looked to the right at the window of Mother's room. The constant flashes of lightning lit Mother sitting in the window, her hair blowing like angry snakes.

The voice kept up its cries, "Hettie! Come to me, Hettie!" Colo-

nel Posey stood on the brick walk below.

I screamed, "MOMMA, HE DOESN'T WANT YOU. HE WANTS HETTIE!"

Mother didn't look at me—she just pushed away from the window, and fell. She seemed to float, falling slowly like a huge white feather, the nightgown wrapped tightly around her. When she smashed against the walk, it sounded like thunder.

The storm abruptly stopped. I felt cold.

The Colonel had disappeared. I watched Mother leave the silent body on the walk and run to Poppa near the stable—they blurred, and then were gone.

I clutched my arms, turned away from the window—the water is gone—then dropped slowly to the floor, rocked myself, and cried, so softly only the moon could hear.

Harrison County Jail

Hungry
by
Joy Kirchgessner

In 1809, the first jail was built in Corydon. Nothing elaborate, just a small log building with iron bars on the openings that served as windows and a door. No electricity. No running water. A holding pen out back provided temporary quarters for unclaimed livestock. Depending on the severity of the crime, punishment was carried out through fines, public whippings while tied to a post or death by hanging. Everyone got to watch.

My great great great grandpa was the first sheriff. Fortunately, he owned the livery stable, too. It didn't pay enough to work only as the sheriff. The salary came from fines and whatever the town could contribute. Somebody had to take the job, keep the peace from time to time. Most of the time it was peaceful. Oh, you'd get a few problems, a drunk and disorderly now and then, husband and wife fighting, disputes over land or ownership of livestock. Generally, disputes were resolved and no one was locked up, whipped or hung. But there was one very strange story that was passed down through the family.

One summer evening, a local farmer stepped outside his back door because he heard his hens causing a commotion in the chicken house. In panic, they cackled loudly and made thumping noises as they hit the walls. Something was after them. So he grabbed his gun and went to the chicken house fully expecting to catch a fox. As he slowly cracked open the door, chickens flew at the gap trying to escape. To his surprise he caught a glimpse of a brutish-looking stranger and flung the door open wide and backed away a few steps. More chickens flew out the door in a frenzy to get away.

"All right mister, get outa there or I'll shoot ya!," the farmer said.

The being stepped out of the shadows.

The farmer shuffled back a few steps again. The ghastly stranger's wiry gray hair hung below his shoulders. Egg yolk, blood, straw and feathers clung to his long, bristly beard. His eyes were deep-

set and yellowish-green. He wore raggedy clothes, his hands were calloused, his feet bare and black with filth. Thick, sallow finger and toenails jutted out to form animal-like, claw-shaped points.

In a guttural voice the stranger said, *"Hungry."*

The farmer froze for barely a moment. The stranger seemed a bit feral or daft so he kept his gun aimed at him. "Mister, ifin you had asked I would a fed ya. But you gone and killed half a my best hens."

The man walked towards the farmer and reached out for him. He said, with more urgent guttural intensity: *"Huungry."* That one word chilled the farmer to the bone.

The farmer, not really wanting to kill a man, especially one possibly deranged from hunger, turned the butt of the gun around quickly, and with a single blow, landed a solid strike on the man's head and knocked him cold. He bound the stranger's hands and feet with rope. Using his horse, he winched the man up onto his wagon. Then, the farmer hitched the horse to the wagon, laid his gun on the seat beside himself and headed for Corydon.

The last of the evening light was fading when he pulled up in front of the livery stable and found the sheriff.

"Got somethin' here for ya, Sheriff."

Grandpa grabbed a lantern and followed the farmer out to the wagon. The horse was trembling, nervously shuffling, wanting to bolt.

The thief lay unconscious in the wagon.

"Caught me a chicken thief." The farmer said matter-of-factly. "Had to hit him on the head. He was comin' at me and he looked kinda crazy. Didn't want to take no chances."

Grandpa knew the farmer and judged him believable.

They both leaned over the side of the wagon with the lantern. The stranger's mouth limply hung open. He moaned and moved slightly.

"Well, he's still alive," Grandpa said. "What a mess. . .you know him?"

"Never seen him before in my life." The farmer shook his head. "Ever seen any teeth like that on a human bein? Looks more like a wolf's or a dog's."

"Yep. Looks like he's lived pretty rough."

"Pull your wagon on over to the jail. It's getting late, so we'll get him locked up before he comes to and straighten all this out in the

morning."

The farmer did as he was asked but kept his gun handy.

Grandpa unlocked the door to the cell. "I got an occupant in the cell right now but I don't think he'll mind the company. He's too drunk to care. Started a ruckus at the tavern."

A man lying on the only cot mumbled but didn't wake.

Grandpa came around to the rear of the wagon and said to the farmer, "You take the feet and I'll take the shoulders. Lay him on the floor. He'll be all right. He can sleep it off, too. I'll leave the ropes on him."

He then secured the cell door. The farmer left for home and so did Grandpa.

First light the next morning, Grandma made breakfast for the prisoners. It was part of the duties of the sheriff—well, ends up a chore for his wife—to prepare meals. We were told that Grandma always cooked the best eggs, homemade sausage, gravy and biscuits. She put a couple of heaping plates in a basket. Grandpa carrying the basket, started off towards the jail whistling a tune and jingling the cell key.

Grandpa neared the cell door and cheerily said, "Up an' atem, boys. Breakfast is ser— ???" And he dropped the basket. Through the cell door—he saw the stranger kneeling over the poor drunk on the dirt floor. Blood everywhere. He had killed the poor drunk and ripped his belly open. He held the heart in his hands and was eating it. The wretch stopped chewing and looked up at Grandpa and said, *"Hungry."*

Well, Grandpa couldn't believe his eyes. He ran to the livery stable, got his gun, knocked on some doors in town to rally help, and came back to the jail. The stranger was still feeding on the poor drunk. Grandpa unlocked the door— two or three men rushed in and grabbed the stranger and pinned him to the ground. He struggled and tried to bite them as they held him. Seeing that he had gotten out of the ropes, someone brought some chain—they used it to secure him to the cell bars.

Let me tell you, everyone was in a bit of a shock by the time they got the drunk's body out and locked the cell door. The whole town thought that maybe the stranger had rabies. Rabies is a terrible thing and there was no cure, no treatment . . . at that time anyway.

Some folks call it dumb rabies. Makes an animal lose its mind. It just starts staggering, foaming at the mouth, grunting and growling, staring straight into nowhere.

They sent for a judge and a short trial was held—held right at the jail—in fact, they never took the stranger out of the cell. The judge sentenced him to hang the next day from a nearby tree on Cherry Street. And the whole time, that thief never said a word . . . only struggled against those chains and grunted and growled.

Come hanging day, the whole town showed up to watch. They hauled that thief-murderer out of the cell and onto the back of a horse-drawn wagon; the wagon was pulled under the tree. They stood him up and cinched the noose around his neck.

The local preacher read from Psalm 23. "Yea though I walk through the valley of the shadow of death, I will fear no evil; for thou art with me; thy rod and thy staff they comfort me, thou preparest a table before me in the presence of mine enemies." After the prayer, he asked the stranger, "Any last words?"

"*Huuungry*," growled the condemned man, and he threw his head back and howled like a wolf.

The noose cut the howl in half as the driver smacked the horse with the reins and rolled out from under the man. He swung from the creaking limb. A few kicks and jerks and it was over.

No one wanted him buried in *their* cemetery so he was buried out behind the jail in the livestock pen, as there were only a couple of unclaimed goats in it at the time. They were herded over to a corner while two men dug a grave.

That night from the livery stable, Grandpa heard the goats bleating strange-like. . .in a way that he knew they were alarmed. He arrived just in time to get a glimpse of something running away in the moonlight. Didn't get a clear look. Only thing is, he swore he heard someone say, "*Hungry!*"

The Courthouse

The Lady with the Mona Lisa Smile

by
Teddi Robinson

A typical Sunday: go to church, Grandma comes for lunch and a visit, and then a drive in the country or, like this Sunday, through Corydon.

At 10, I considered Corydon just a sleepy little town. There were never many people walking around on Sunday, but I always enjoyed looking at the buildings on the square. I thought they were impressive but cold. Dad told me the small square building with the gray stone was once the state capitol of Indiana. The other larger structure with the brown stone was, and still is, the courthouse. *I would have liked to have lived when Indiana was admitted to statehood. I bet it was exciting.*

Dad spoke, "Thedy, did you know that I used to work in the courthouse?"

"No," I answered. "I was wondering about the things that the building could tell us."

"Then, I guess I can tell you about the ghost I saw." said Dad.

Oh boy! A ghost story! A true experience for my dad. I can hardly wait for him to start. He's the greatest story teller in the world. . . .

During the depression you took any job that was offered at whatever price they wanted to pay.

Not many men wanted a night watchman, janitor, maintenance job. Just too much responsibility for $6.00 per week. But, it was a job and I was glad to get it.

The two men I worked with were good, honest, hardworking men. Smith worked from 7:00 a.m. till 3:00 p.m., I worked 3:00 p.m. till 11:00 p.m. and Callahan worked the 11:00 p.m. till 7:00 a.m. shift. We always came in a few minutes early to discuss any jobs that needed fixing. Also, we might stay a few minutes late to help. Some things needed four hands instead of two.

One afternoon, I got to work early.

Smith said, "John, Callahan is ill. I hope you don't mind, but I'd like you to work the first four hours and I'll come in at 3 o'clock for the other four hours. Okay?"

"Will we get paid extra?"

"I'm not sure, but it'll keep his job, otherwise they'll hire someone else to take his place."

I thought a minute. After all, I might be ill sometime and I felt sure these two men would do the same for me. "Okay; his wife just had a miscarriage and I'm sure he hasn't gotten over his loss. I'll do this for one week, then he'll have to get his act together."

The first two nights were the same humdrum shifts they always were. But the third night made my hair stand on end.

I started down the hall and caught a glimpse of someone or something moving very fast toward the stairs. So I hurried to the steps as fast as I could with my "billy club" in my hand.

"What's a billy club?" I asked.

Dad replied, "It looked like a baseball bat except the top was fatter and the club was shorter."

"What was it for?"

"Making us feel tough, I guess."

Anyway, when I got to the stairs, there she was: Callahan's wife. She looked very pretty with her long black hair and laughing blue eyes. Then I saw the blood stain on the gorgeous blue dress. I asked, "In the name of the Father, the Son, and the Holy Ghost, what do you want? How did you get in and do you need help?"

She didn't say a word, Just gave me a Mona Lisa smile and disappeared.

To say I was frightened is the understatement of the year.

I didn't say anything to Smith. He would have thought I'd stolen a nap and dreamed what I'd seen.

Callahan came to work the next evening.

Around 1:00 a.m., my phone rang. It was Callahan.

"John, I need to leave. Will you come relieve me?"

"Give me a few minutes."

"Thanks."

I got there a little before 3:00 and I have never seen anyone look like Callahan before or after.

Callahan's eyes were as wide as they could get without popping out of his head. His hair was standing straight up, like he had run his hand through it. He was shaking from head to foot as if he were using a jackhammer. His face was whiter than white. I knew he was in shock but waited for him to speak.

"Thank God, you're here. I need to leave."

"What happened? Did someone try to break in?"

"Oh, John, I've seen something that I can't explain. I saw Lisa with a blood stain on her favorite dress. I'll call her mother to see if she's okay."

"So, Lisa's at her mother's?"

"Yes, she left four days ago. We had a terrible fight. Ever since she lost the baby, she's been like a different person. I can't do anything to please her, and all she wants to do is sit and cry."

"Did you tell the doctor?"

"No, I tried to get her to go, but she refused."

"It's time to make the rounds and I think you should go with me. Then you can leave."

We started the rounds and...guess what? We glimpsed something or someone in the hall heading for the stairs. I rushed toward it, but Callahan hung back.

Just as before, there she stood, beautiful as always, except for the blood stain.

Again, I asked, "In the name of the Father, the Son, and the Holy Ghost, what do you want?"

She smiled the Mona Lisa smile and pointed at Callahan.

He screamed and fainted.

I revived him and finished the rounds. When I got back to the maintenance room, he was still there, still shaking and pale.

"Okay, Callahan, what really happened? I saw her the other night but she didn't point her finger. That finger pointed directly at you."

"I can't go on living like this. I see her in all the rooms at home. Always unexpected. She always points that finger at me. I never know

when she'll show up or where.

"The first night I didn't show up for work, I was ill. She had nagged me, for most of the day. The same thing over and over. I wanted to scream, *Just shut up*. I can't help that she lost the baby. How was I to know that she wasn't strong enough to ride in the car to church? I couldn't take a better road—there wasn't one. I'm sorry that I couldn't get a better job or live in a nicer home. John, I was doing the best I could. Why, oh why couldn't she understand that I was upset, too? I wanted the baby as much as she did...maybe a little more. I had big plans for our child. We would go fishing and play games. I was looking forward to teaching him all the things my dad had taught me.

"I don't have any idea of what happened. I found myself standing over her, holding the butcher knife, and she was on the floor with the blood stain on her dress. They had just finished planting the evergreens in front of the courthouse. I buried her under the evergreens after midnight. I've told everyone that Lisa made good her threat to leave me and go to her mother's.

"John, what do I do now? She's a worse nag in death than she was in life. What can I do?"

"The first thing is to call the sheriff and you turn yourself in. Then you'll need a lawyer."

The trial didn't last long and Callahan was convicted. He was sentenced to die in the electric chair.

I quit the job.

They say that she can still be seen on beautiful moonlit nights, around midnight. She still stalks the halls and the staircase of the courthouse.

"John, is that true or did you make it up?" my mother asked.
"It's true alright. The story is all there in the courthouse records."
Buildings do have stories to tell . . . if they could talk.

Governor Hendricks House

Music of the Soul
by
Glenda Mills

Megan put the last of her Winnie the Pooh figurines on the shelf above the sink. Their bright faces lifted her spirits every time she saw them, and she did spend a lot of time in the kitchen. It seemed old habits were hard to break. She still couldn't get used to cooking for one instead of two. She'd had the same problem as the children left home, gradually adjusting from five to four to three. Now, Kevin was gone, taken from her by a heart attack.

The moving company had unloaded the last of her boxes yesterday, and she'd spent most of the night unpacking. She might as well do something constructive with all the hours she spent not sleeping these days. The house was small, but there was plenty of room for just her. She and Kevin had spent most of their life together in Indianapolis, but after he died, Megan felt she needed a change of surroundings, a new life with a slower pace; Corydon seemed like the perfect town to start over.

The grandfather clock in the living room chimed twelve times. Megan had to be at work at the Hendricks House at one o'clock, so she made a tuna sandwich, washed up her dishes, and walked outside. It was a hot muggy July afternoon. Her air-conditioned car looked terribly inviting, but the walk would be better for her and for the ozone layer. Besides, Elliott Street wasn't far from work.

Five hours later, Megan locked the door on Governor Hendricks' mansion. The Roberts family had been her last tour of the day. She considered going home, but there were two really good arguments against that idea. For starters, going back to a lonely house was no fun. Besides, the outdoor sauna she had endured on her way to work had not abated at all. In fact, if what she'd felt in the open doorway was any indication, it had actually gotten worse. She opted for a diet soda, a comfortable chair, and a book about the history of Corydon. She'd get in some study time, wait for the temperature to drop, and get a bite to eat on the way back to Elliott. The combination of reading, sitting,

and resting quickly led to napping.

By the time she woke up, it was dusk. Corydon wasn't exactly the crime capitol of the country. Still, Megan didn't really want to walk home in the dark. She hurried to the closet to get her purse. She was walking down the hall on the second floor when she heard the low, mournful sound of a harmonica coming from the big room downstairs. Quietly, she made her way to the room, but by the time she got to the doorway, the music had stopped. Obviously, the stress of life and the lack of supper were playing tricks on her mind. She took a deep breath and turned to leave.

She had only taken a few steps before she heard the music again. This time, she followed the sound to the foot of the stairs. There was no one there. She listened as the tune faded and began again. Now it was in the hallway above her head. There was no way she was following some invisible troubadour upstairs. She ran down the hall, opened the door and didn't look back. She'd gone three blocks before the pounding of her heart and the pain in her side grabbed her attention, and she slowed her pace.

Since the Hendricks House was not open for tours on Mondays, she spent her morning at the library doing research into the history of the governor's mansion. Something had happened the night before; that she was sure of. Exactly what, she didn't know. By noon, she'd only found one report of ghostly sightings. Apparently, a large, white horse had been seen galloping through the front door. Governor Hendricks had died in the house, but there were no reported sightings of him or any mention that he ever played the harmonica. There was some mention of the "colored" people using the house as a meeting place for church services, but no mention of any apparitions connected to their presence. After hours of searching, she found herself even more confused than before.

On Tuesday, Megan left for work early. She wanted to tell Stella about what had happened on Sunday night. Stella was one of those people that you couldn't help but like, and Megan felt sure that even if Stella didn't know what was going on, she would believe her story. Sure enough, Stella's yellow Volkswagen was already in the parking

lot when Megan arrived.

She followed the scent of fresh-brewed coffee and found Stella in the small room the employees had claimed as both a lounge and a kitchen, sipping her morning caffeine rush from a cup that read "Someone I know went to Corydon, and all I got was this lousy mug." Megan made herself a cup of blackberry tea and sat down across from Stella.

"So, how did Sunday go? I hope it wasn't too soon to leave you to fend for yourself around here." Stella grinned over the top of her cup and winked.

"Actually, something did happen on Sunday that I need to talk to you about."

"Don't tell me. Old man Kepler came over with a single red carnation and asked you out for dinner."

"No, no one came with flowers. Whose old man Kepler, anyway?"

"He lives down on Water Street. He's harmless, really, but as soon as he knows there's a new girl in town, he comes a-calling. Just tell him politely that you're not interested, and he'll leave you be."

"Okay, that's good to know. Now, back to what happened Sunday. It was around dusk, and I was getting ready to leave when I heard music—harmonica music—coming from different rooms in the house, but there wasn't anyone here but me. I checked all the rooms downstairs, but. . . ."

Stella put her cup down on the table and held up her hand. "You don't have to tell me no more. I've heard it, too. You just had your first encounter with Jeremiah."

Megan took another sip of tea and waited. No matter how unsettling this Jeremiah character was, she was relieved to find that not only did Stella believe her, but she had "met" him, too.

"You see," Stella continued, "at one time this building was used by black people in the area as a church."

"I read about that yesterday."

"Yeah, well, what you probably didn't see written down anywhere was what happened here on a Sunday evening during one of those meetings. You see, there were some white boys in town who thought it would be real funny to scare them 'colored' people right in

the middle of a revival, so they snuck inside and threw rocks down the stairs. Then they moaned and shrieked and carried on. The black folk thought there were ghosts in the building, and they panicked. The boys watched from a window at the top of the steps, laughing at all the people running from the doors and climbing out the windows."

"That was a mean trick."

"The only written account I've ever seen called the boys fun-loving. Today, the boys would be punished by the law, especially considering what happened next, but those were different times."

"What did happen?" Megan took another sip of her tea, which was now cold, and waited.

Stella looked away for a moment before continuing. "In all the excitement, a little boy named Isaac, who was only five years old, got separated from his parents. Once things settled down, his family realized he was missing and started looking for him. The whole church community went through the woods, calling for him. His father got to thinking that maybe the boy was scared of the voices—that maybe he thought he was still hearing the ghosts from the church—so he began to play his harmonica. He knew if his boy heard the music, he would know it was safe to come out of hiding."

Megan, feeling the sting in her eyes, blinked away the tears.

"They never did find little Isaac, but Jeremiah kept on playing. He would come here every evening and fill this house with music, hoping his boy would find his way back. I reckon he's still searching, waiting to cross over until he and Isaac can go together. I know this is going to sound strange, but sometimes, when I hear his music, it reminds me that there are people on the other side, waiting for me to be with them, and it gives me comfort. You probably think I'm touched, but. . . ."

This time it was Megan who lifted her hand to interrupt. "No, Stella, I don't. In fact, it makes perfect sense to me."

Star Cleaners

The Prince Albert Coat

by
Bonnie Abraham

I stared at the coat my husband had brought home from Star Cleaners. It was a strange coat—handsome, to be sure—but nothing anyone would wear today. Well, maybe as a costume. It looked like something I had seen before, though. I tried to place just where: Currier and Ives? Dickens' *A Christmas Carol*? No. My father's can of Prince Albert tobacco.

How did it come to be in our cleaning? Well, Matt would have to return it, of course. Nevertheless, I was curious about the owner of such a coat. Maybe he was connected with Hayswood Theater.

I stroked the thick, black wool. There was nothing soft about it. It must be very uncomfortable to wear. I considered checking the pockets, but figured that would be useless. I always check the pockets of our own clothes before sending them out to be cleaned and I was sure the owner had done the same. And the cleaners would have removed anything the owner had missed. The pockets would be empty.

My husband called me from the kitchen and I left the coat hanging on the back of the closet door. No time now to daydream about old coats.

The next morning, Matt took the coat with him when he left for work. I was sorry to see it go. Crazy, I know, but I was curious. I went about my work and tried to forget the whole thing, but by the middle of the morning, I gave up and went to the computer. A little internet surfing told me the coat might be described as a Prince Albert coat – but it wasn't a Prince Albert frock coat. That was longer and skirted—that is, it had a waist seam. The things one can learn on the internet! By that time, I had killed a couple of hours and it was time to put the ham in the oven for dinner and get started on the potato salad. At least now I had a time-frame for my day-dreaming—late 1800's.

Matt had said he didn't know when he would be home for supper. When I had finished the cooking and set the table, I pulled out my knitting. I was just finishing a sleeve when I saw his car lights. I put the sweater away and heard him come in the back door.

"You're not going to believe this," he called as I started to the kitchen.

"Believe what?" I asked.

"That coat. I took it back to Star Cleaners and they said they had never seen it before. They wouldn't take it back." He came into the kitchen carrying the coat and gave me a quick kiss. He broke off a piece of ham from the plate I was carrying to the table. "Looks good."

"So what are we supposed to do with it?"

"Do with what?"

"The coat," I said, pointing to where he had draped it over the back of the chair.

He shrugged. "Give it to Goodwill? I don't know. Whatever you want, I guess." He went to the sink and washed his hands, then sat down at the table and stabbed a slice of ham with his fork. "It's quite a coat. Where do you think it came from?"

It was my turn to shrug. "No idea. Maybe it belongs to some actor or someone who does historical reenactments—like the guys who fight Civil War battles."

"Not Civil War, though," said Matt around a mouthful of potato salad.

"No," I said. "It's too late."

"It's not military."

"That too, but it's the wrong time period altogether. It's late Victorian, or Edwardian."

Matt shrugged again, unimpressed by my new-found knowledge of men's attire. "I have to work tomorrow."

Clearly, the subject was of no more interest to him. "I thought we were going hiking."

"Couldn't pass up the overtime." Same old story.

We finished supper in silence. After washing up, I took the mysterious garment and hung it in the guestroom closet. As I was closing the door, I noticed the back of the coat for the first time. Quickly, I tore away the plastic bag for a better look. A slit, about three inches long, ran horizontally on the left side of the coat. I pulled it out and examined the tear. No. It was a cut. And there was a stain around it. I touched it and my finger came away red.

"Matt! You'd better come see this!"

"Smells like blood," said Matt, when he had examined the evidence. "Why didn't we notice the hole before? And how could it still be wet? It was locked in the truck except when I carried it back into the cleaners."

I stared at my finger. The red was darker now, almost brown. "I think I'm going to be sick."

"Go wash."

We debated calling the police, but the whole thing was just too bizarre. There were too many questions we wouldn't be able to answer.

"I'll call Roberts," said Matt, finally.

Roberts was the jack-of-all-trades who had helped Matt with house repairs when we first moved in and he had been Matt's go-to man ever since. Well, mine too, if truth be known. Roberts knows something about everything. Sometimes, I was sure Matt invented problems just so he could ask Roberts over and hear his stories.

"Appears to be old," said Roberts, as he brushed his gnarled fingers over the rough fabric. "Not made like things today. Made to last."

Roberts is pretty old, himself, I thought. Made to last, like the coat. I wondered just what his age really was.

"Odd the blood's not dried by now," said our advisor. He turned away from the garment and rubbed the white stubble on his chin. "Something's not right about this." He paused, turned back to the jacket for a moment. "This cut, now, this was a killing stab—and I know these buttons. Mighty strange."

"Strange?" asked Matt. "They're just brass buttons."

"Look close. I've only seen ones like 'em in a picture I have of my dad and a friend of his." He ran fingers through his thin white hair, causing it to stand on end. "I need to take a look at that picture again."

"You know they're the same from an old picture?" said Matt. He sounded as incredulous as I felt.

"You'll see," said Roberts. "I'll go get it. Be back in about 15 minutes."

Roberts left and returned with the picture. It was amazingly

clear, and because of a strange quirk of shadow and light, the distinctive circular design of the buttons stood out in detail. They were an exact match to the buttons on the coat in our closet. The coat in the picture appeared to be the same style and color, too.

"Who is he?" I asked.

"Was," said Roberts. "I never knew his name, that I remember, but he disappeared not long after that picture was taken. My dad used to tell me the story every time he looked at it. It was always when Mother wasn't around. I think that had something to do with his never telling me his friend's name." He pulled out a chair and sat down at the table where Matt and I had gone for coffee while we waited. I got him a mug and poured, while he continued telling his story.

"Mother knew about the picture. Once, when Dad was away, she came across it as she was cleaning. She didn't know I was home and I saw her stroke the picture with her finger—gentle and loving-like—and it wasn't my father's face she touched.

"There was a fire in town. Let me see. It would have been . . ." He sipped coffee as he paused to think. "1892. Took out a house and, I think, a grocery. The house belonged to a Carter Larkins. My dad's friend disappeared the same night. They'd had an argument over something that morning. After I saw Mother with the picture, I always suspected it was over her. Dad's friend sent word he was going to the church, just past the Larkins' place, and Dad was to meet him. Dad thought he was going to apologize so he went, but his friend never showed."

"But how did the coat get to Star Cleaners?" asked Matt, "and why did it come to us?"

Roberts shook his head and took another sip of coffee. "The Larkins land sold. Donahue built a restaurant on it and the Sunshine Hatchery stood on part of it. There was another fire in the same spot in '48 – burned Donahue's and the hatchery. Donahue's rebuilt. It's where the Mexican restaurant is now, but the hatchery didn't rebuild. That land's where Star Cleaners sits now."

"You're joshin' me, right?" said Matt.

Roberts' clear blue eyes never blinked as he stared Matt down. "Nope. There used to be rumors about the hatchery. They said there was a ghost used to prowl the place – wearin' an old Prince Albert

coat, and with a knife in his back. I never much believed it but Dad wouldn't go in the place. Always sent me. I never made the connection with Dad's friend." He shook his head sadly and took a sip of coffee. "Murdered. Who'd a thought it?"

"But how did we get the coat?" I asked.

Roberts scratched at his chin stubble. "Now that's a puzzle. Maybe it knew you'd fetch me. I never had any reason to go to the cleaners, myself."

"You're saying the coat wanted to get to you?" asked Matt. "Why?"

"Only one reason I can think of," said Roberts. "It wants justice. It thinks I might know who killed him—or should know."

"But wouldn't the killer be dead by now?" I asked.

Roberts set his cup carefully on the table. His hand was shaking. "The killer is, but his son isn't. My dad went to meet his friend that night—but he wasn't expecting an apology. He went to kill him. It's the only thing that makes sense. He was the only one who knew where his friend was.

"The messenger who sent word for your father to meet him knew," said Matt.

Roberts shook his head. "The messenger was my mother."

Presbyterian Church (Wright Center)

Old CPC
by
J. Baumgartle

Morgan's Raiders had made a name for themselves, but whether it was an honorable name, after all the things he asked of his men, or not, this battle was ending.

John Anderson surfaced once more from the darkness he fell into sometimes. War was the background of his dreams: the thrall of explosions, their deafening vacuum that forced him to open his mouth; chewing smoke, swallowing it; like his brother beside him, trying to mount a charge through chest-high brambles; the whap of bullets impacting all around them; tripping over a body. . . .

He knew he'd been hit, and dragged away, and ended up inside, on the floor of a church. Corydon Presbyterian, they told him. Presbyterian women wiping at him, offering him water, blankets, assurances— How many days had he been here, anyway–two? three? forever?

His eyelids were weighted with light, and his mind rushed to summon courage for what he knew was coming. He strained toward a pan that wasn't there. A wood floor, yes. A clean, waxed floor. He lay back, confused. Where was the pain? They'd sent for painkiller. Maybe it had come. For some reason, he wasn't worried.

Rest . . . rest. Rest is best. A chuckle wanted out, at the stupidity of rhyme, but you don't laugh with your insides full of lead. He glanced over at Josh, whose leg had been about blown off. Only Josh wasn't there. No one was.

John Anderson stood up. Hands dangled beside him, his hands, as they were before the war. He was dressed like at home, too, wearing his favorite boots. He could see the floor through them. —It was true, then. He hadn't made it.

Time sort of stepped back a while as he tried to figure things out. He had a presence; thin as it was, he recognized it. But this place . . . he wasn't sure what to make of it. Shelves lined the walls, with

assorted brick-a-brack on them. Toys, books, clothing, a cabinet for a clerk to sit behind. Not a general store, no necessities or food. Not a home, no bed or stove or anything. For some reason, ordinary tools were on display in a glass case.

Perhaps the double doors. . . . They opened easily (at least, to him), and he was in a church, after all. Light streamed through the colored-glass pictures, showed him the altar, and the pulpit with an open Bible on it. A flag stood at each side of the sanctuary. He found himself touching one, holding up the free corner to see what was embroidered on it. A cross; well, sure. The other, he soon realized, was not Confederate. More like Union. But look at all those stars—by his count, fifty-two. Generations. Generations. Generations. . . . This place, in this time. God had brought him to see it; the reason would come clear.

His spirit returned to the south room it had waked in. Late afternoon sun cast colorful beams across the floor. In wonder, he sat himself down on the clerk's chair. No need to hurry now. All had happened that could happen. —No more problems, he thought, sighing with a mixture of relief and regret.

Life had seemed difficult enough for the last few years. True, he'd had advantages on earth that many people didn't, such as loving parents, a close family, and a brother that took him into the business of constructing houses and barns. Having a trade had enabled him to start his own life. He shook his head. Some life he'd made. He'd married Daley, without knowing her very long. Surely, no man had ever taken a bride more flighty and irresponsible. In a year's time, she had charmed and embarrassed, flirted and sworn-off flirting repeatedly, and decimated their bank account. He had hoped, with the advent of children, that she would settle down to motherhood.

If she ever did, it was in some other place, with some other man. Daley was a lost cause. —Maybe not to God, but to him.

Edward and he had differed in opinion about the need for war, but when Edward decided to enlist, John had gone with him, unwilling to see his brother go off alone. —Edward; where was he? Without thinking, Jonathan spun around, frenzy taking a moment to subside into reason. His brother, like everyone else, was lost, either to the cause or to time. Nowhere on this earth to turn to find him, or any of them. He

determinedly resigned himself to the fact, called up memories, one by one, to mourn them, and to lay them to rest in his heart.

—It all seemed so pointless, now. All those men who had fought for the Confederacy (or the Union), all the families that had been disrupted, they didn't exist anymore. If anything had been gained. . . .

Daylight eventually returned. John was bowed contemplatively in the chair, when he heard a key rattle in the lock, and the doors creak open. His first thought was to scramble into hiding. Then he recalled the influence daylight was supposed to have on spirits, and merely conformed to the background. Two people, a young woman and a middle-aged one entered. The younger one was expecting a baby. They were both startlingly dressed, as if in men's clothing, clothing that fit closely without dealing in illusion.

"The computer isn't much," the elder lady informed, "but it does the job. You say you've used this program before?" The younger of the two followed around the counter, to see what was being explained. "Just a minute; it takes a while for it to come up, sometimes . . . there." Her fingers pecked at a panel of lettering, and a slate lighted up. "You see, the entries go here. . . ."

"Yes; I have used this before," the younger one politely intervened. "Let's see; did you want to log in the description of each purchase?" Her hands, incredibly, made numbers line themselves up in columns, then scatter over the page.

"That would be fine, Lora. As long as we have enough to identify returns, we're good. I'll be back in a couple of months. — When did you say your baby is due?"

"September 7, if Kyle Jonathan Anderson agrees." She patted the bulge under her clothing, and smiled warmly.

The other woman returned her smile, gathering her purse and jacket. "Hopefully, he does. —Got to go. You have my number. . ." The young lady, Lora, produced a card to show her, which was acknowledged with a nod.

"Let me know if you need anything," and she hurried off.

Jonathan was stunned. An apparent namesake. Could it possibly be a descendent of his? Perhaps. Surely, he had not been

awakened to mere coincidence. But then, his brother Edward may have survived, and one of his progeny had elected to honor the long lost uncle.

He rose from his seat, hurriedly, to allow the young mother to sit down, which she did, gracefully, considering her condition. She opened her pocketbook, and sorted through some scraps of crinkled paper. Her hands were smooth, with a rich skin tone, though one nail was broken. An image of pale, pink-tipped fingers came to him, his wife's hands as they appeared when she removed her gloves. He could see the gloves, lying where they had been tossed, white and hand-shaped. Empty. —This was better, these active, warm hands that would handle a baby.

Sometime during the morning, he was startled by a metallic squeal from outside. Young voices, rowdy and giggling, preceded their owners' clambering footfalls up the steps. It was like a rush of wind as they came in and spread everywhere, touching, browsing, commenting. The young woman Lora rose to meet them, and made her way among them, answering questions, offering directions and at times, leading them to the desk. He wanted to admonish the youngsters, caution them about bumping or tripping a woman in her condition, but Lora remained cheerfully unfazed by the chaos, which ended suddenly.

"Everybody back to the bus. It's eleven-thirty!" Jonathan Anderson's insubstantial chin dropped. A black man. No way to explain it. Neither his speech, nor manner, nor his dress distinguished him from the rude children. A black man in charge! He commenced herding the youngsters towards the doorway, which was suddenly packed with those not wanting to be the last one out.

Welcome silence filled the room. The girl, Lora, went around tidying the shop, left the room for a couple of minutes, then came back and sat before the lighted slate. A few taps, a chime, and the slate went blank.

The sound of steps being taken, two at a time.

"Hi, hon! How'd it go?" This, spoken somewhat breathlessly, as the man hurried to receive Lora's embrace.

It was, for all the world, as though Jonathan was seeing himself enter the room. The same build, bordering on lanky, clothed in— whatever garb that was called—the same face, with a look on it he

would gladly have slipped into.

"Fine," she replied, her head nestled against him as if this was the "Fine" of it.

"Good, good. Those teenagers give you a hard time?"

She grinned and pushed away a little. "You know better than that, Jon Anderson. I manage you, don't I?

"Ah. Yes. Yes, you do. —I don't suppose you could manage the time to go to lunch? I have to be at work at 1:00."

"You know I can."

They fairly beamed at each other, and were gone almost before he could miss them. The ghost braced against the counter would have swallowed tears if any had come. —There was more hope in the world than he had ever dreamed of. . . .

He shook his head regretfully. He wanted more than anything to stay, follow their lives, see the new grandson, but it was time to let them make their own memories. All mysteries would eventually be revealed to these loved ones, as they were now revealed to him.

—Lives, beautiful lives. He was a part of them, would always be—along with someone he'd given up on. —Release and assurance. Maybe these awaited all spirits, including hers, but Jonathan Anderson intended to put his own words to them.

And Elsewhere . . . .

Love Song For Pythias
by
Marian Allen

This story is dedicated to the memory of Tom Schickel, but the character of "Tom" is not meant to be the real Tom, nor his history Tom's history.

I wouldn't have seen the shaky letters if the sun hadn't hit just so. They glossed the dresser mirror, clear but shiny, like furniture wax or margarine or the oil of a fingertip.

Elinir

Butchie, my new landlord, waved a hand toward the glass as if he could wipe it clean by psychic power. "Sorry, man. One of the middle-schoolers must have got up here."

Butchie owned this building on Chestnut Street. He ran a shoe and leather goods repair business in the front, and Pythias Art Gallery and Coffee Shop in the back. He had offered me the top floor of his building for pocket change and my services as a janitor. From the time school let out until the place closed around midnight, Pythias was full of people—people who had too much trouble running their own lives to try to run anyone else's.

He said, "You got cleaning stuff? You want me to—"

"No, it's cool." I was calculating how to get a photograph of it. If I could catch the way it was only visible depending on the way it was looked at. . . .

Photography. That's what I do. Weddings, parties, portraits, product shots for advertising, stock shots, art—I didn't make a lot, but I did what I wanted. Mostly.

Apart from the autograph of a chick who couldn't spell her own name, my new place was clean, but shabby. Cheap, which was its major appeal. No, its major appeal was the coffee house on the floor below, telling me that I was not alone, no matter what I felt like. The apartment had come furnished, which was another plus. The furniture seemed to have been salvaged from thrift stores and yard sales. I liked that, too. I didn't need to get a life. I had a life, as anybody could see by the nicks and scratches and cigarette burns and water rings on my furniture, not to mention someone's name smeared across my mirror.

Getting some shots of *Elinir* took me a couple of hours. I set up lights to see which angle made the sheen most visible, but I also had to do it all from an angle that wouldn't show the lights or me in the mirror. I was using a real camera—not a digital, I mean—so I wouldn't know how the shots came out until I had developed them. Part of the excitement.

I had a quick cheese sandwich and cold canned tomato soup and joined the clientele downstairs at Pythias. They were a colorful crew, from the youngest middle-schooler to the oldest insomniac, poets and painters and philosophers and just plain loudmouths. I snapped pictures of them playing chess and poker, strumming guitars and improvising on the piano, of Butchie mixing coffee drinks and Italian sodas, and of faces full of laughter, anger, boredom, pain.

After Butchie herded the last patron out, I earned my keep: locked the door and stained-glass windows, emptied the ashtrays, threw away the paper trash, dusted, swept, washed the dishes, turned out the lights and went upstairs.

That was the best time for developing photographs. I would send the color stuff away—the labs could do it cheaper than I could—but I had set up a darkroom in a walk-in closet for the black and white stuff. The newer automated developers didn't know what to do with black and white—it came out green or purple or some crazy thing. Besides, I wanted to develop *Elinir* myself. It would take a delicate touch, some trial-and-error and plenty of dumb luck to get a good print of that.

The shots of the Pythias gang came out great, but I must have had a light source I hadn't accounted for when I took the *Elinir* pictures. Every one of them had a nimbus that bleached out the letters. Well, I had known it was a tricky shot. One of the great and equally one of the most frustrating things about photography is how random your success is. Kind of like love, that way.

I emerged from the darkroom and lit a cigarette, thinking about turning in.

"Tom!" It was a woman's voice, distant. *Downstairs? No. Couldn't be.* Besides, a voice sounds different sandwiched between the walls of a building than it does out in the open. "Tom. . . ! Take my picture, Tom." The voice was light, tentatively hopeful. *One of the*

high-schoolers, out after curfew? I'm as vain as the next guy, but not vain enough to think a teen girl might have a crush on me. More than one had gotten a crush on having her picture taken, though, so I went to the window and raised the sash and leaned out. There weren't any screens; I was able to see below right up to the doorway as well as across the street and for blocks on either side. *Nobody in sight. Hiding between the buildings?* I put out my cigarette, got my camera and snapped some pictures of the empty street.

Now I wasn't sleepy any more.

Singing a song about wine, I poured myself a shot of Tequila. It wasn't until the buzz hit the pit of my stomach that I remembered I hadn't eaten since my soup and sandwich. I remedied that with a package of peanut-butter-on-crackers and topped it off with another shot.

"Tom! Tom!" The voice chimed gently.

Suddenly tired out, I shuffled to the window and peered blearily at the view with nobody in it.

"You're not funny!" I shouted into the night.

I closed the window and leaned my head against the frame, wondering if I had imagined the voice, so clear and sweet in my memory. *Nobody.* With a deep sigh, I pushed away... then looked closer. I huffed again against the pane, and there it was, fading as the fog of my breathing faded.

Elinir.

The next day, I cleaned all the windows, mirrors and the glass on my framed photos. I dusted every flat surface. I wasn't having some joker leave a mark on my living space, like a brand or a logo. The name and the voice were firmly connected in my mind. This was all some elaborate practical joke cooked up by my Pythias friends to make life interesting.

But nobody acted right for that. Nobody asked me about how I slept or if anything unusual had happened in the night, and the all-but-invisibility of the name was just WAY too subtle for the comedians in the coffee house crowd.

So if it wasn't a joke, what was it?

When you start looking for odd behavior in any random segment

of population, you're bound to find it, especially in a group that prides itself on odd behavior. I didn't accomplish anything by trying to scope out which girl had hidden herself near my window except to inspire one guy, small and wiry and manic, to remind me that the brunette in the corner was his best friend, and I should look elsewhere.

I asked if any of them knew anybody named Eleanor but, apart from one wise guy who opened his history book and showed me a picture of Eleanor Roosevelt, nobody did.

Somebody suggested a walk, and I went along, taking pictures of anything anybody suggested: "That rusty staircase," "The library clock from straight below it," "The crack between those two buildings, where somebody dumped all those glass bottles." I got so interested, I almost forgot my original goal was to finish the roll with last night's empty street on it.

Back at Pythias, I couldn't wait. I unlocked the door to my staircase and locked and bolted it behind me.

I wrote *film* on my shopping list and locked myself in the darkroom.

Some of the shots on that roll were really good. I'd scan them and put them up on my web site. But the ones of the empty street. . . . They were sharp, with geometric shapes of light and shadow, impersonal and inorganic, except . . . every one of those empty street ones had a bright nimbus in them, directly under my window.

I hung the prints up to dry and reminded myself I needed film. When I looked at my shopping list, I saw I had already written it down. I also saw an item that I hadn't written, that hadn't been there before I went into the darkroom, in pencil so faint it barely left a mark: *Elinir.*

Time for a Drink Yourself Sober Special. I tucked a fifth of peach schnapps into the inside pocket of my jacket, went down into the coffee shop, got an espresso in a big mug and cut it with the schnapps. Half an hour later, I was talking philosophy and metaphysics; fifteen minutes after that, I couldn't tell you *what* I was talking about.

Next thing I knew, five of us were upstairs smoking, listening to Janis Joplin and arguing about how to determine how many angels could dance on the head of a pin depending on what kind of dance they were doing—naturally, more could do the twist than the stroll, that stands to reason.

All the time, I was halfway listening for the voice to call me. I never actually heard it, but every so often I would hold up a finger and say, "Hark!" Then we would light some firecrackers I had bought back before July 4th and forgotten about, and throw them out the window.

A couple of times, voices that sounded nothing like the one I remembered would yell startled obscenities. It was highly satisfying.

At some point, everybody else left and I dragged myself to bed.

The voice invaded my sleep. No matter where my unconscious mind took me, that clear, sweet voice penetrated the weirdness or banality or frustration or nightmare, calling softly, "Take my picture, Tom. Take my picture."

In my dream, there was a camera, but it wasn't any of my real cameras, it was one of those big old ones with the accordian front and the tripod and the cloth to cover the photographer's head. It focused on a patch of moonlit wall. The camera stood as if it were bolted to the floor, but I floated around the room, my eyes always turned to where the camera pointed. As I watched—although I had the impression of long minutes passing, this happened very quickly—the moonlight took on the shape of a bright female figure. She wore an ankle-length dress and a shawl, her hair knotted on top of her head. The details were whited out, but my dream self could clearly "see" her look at me and smile.

"Don't move," I told her. "It takes a long time to develop."

"All right, Tom. I don't mind waiting."

I communed with the woman whose features were blurred by light through that unique connection between photographer and photographed. Sometimes I think I never really see people until I look at them through a camera lens. Private people—secret people—display their souls in pictures. When this photographic plate was developed, I would see "Elinir", know her, but the dream faded before that happened.

When I woke, afternoon sunlight streamed through the window, waiting to poke me in the eyeballs. My head throbbed, but my memory of taking that photograph was so strong I didn't care. When I realized the photo session had only been the dream of a picture never shot of a subject that didn't exist with a camera I didn't own, a black depression

settled on me like a soggy quilt.

I took three aspirin and went back to bed, and didn't get up until my stomach growled so loud it woke me from a dreamless stupor.

A shower made me feel slightly better. A cigarette, a cup of coffee and a stale doughnut brought me up to merely groggy and washed-out. I would have gone back to bed, but I couldn't stay in that apartment a minute longer. It seemed full and empty at the same time, companionable and lonely, happy and bereft.

I grabbed my wallet and stumbled out past the Saturday loafers and gloomed my way to the diner on the corner. After three cheeseburgers, a piece of orange cake, a coffee and two refills, I was ready to go back and do some work. This Elinir thing—what was I supposed to do about it? There was nothing I could do about it. My web site needed updating, client emails needed answering, my schedule needed filling in.

One of the reasons I was no longer married was my ability to blind and deafen myself to anything but my work. I did that now, ignoring my awareness of the lonely voice, the insubstantial autographs, the profound sense of loss that underlay my choice.

Although some of my clients made me want to pull my hair out and stuff it down their throats, some of them were great. There was this horse owner who paid me to come down to his mansion outside of Lexington when one of his mares foaled and take baby pictures of the blessed arrival's first two weeks. He threw catered barbecues for fifty and kept open house for all his friends and all the friends of his friends, and I had the run of the place.

Once or Twice in a Lifetime's due date was in early September. The summons came, and I packed my bags and equipment, looking forward to the little bundle of strength and beauty I was going to witness at its beginning—and to the free food and booze.

A sigh, below hearing, softer than a thought, drifted through my soul:

"Ah, Tom, you coming back? You ever coming back?"

"I am," I said aloud. "I am . . . Eleanor."

It was peaceful out in the country, in spite of all the company

coming and going. There was never a half-literate scribble anywhere unexplainable; there was never a voice from nowhere or a dream that broke my heart when I woke up. I sat outside a lot, listening to the gentle noises of the horses and bugs and nightbirds. Sometimes I was still awake when the stablehands got up, and I got a reputation for being an early riser until I confessed.

Two weeks of work and pleasure should have neutralized my memory of Eleanor's vague semi-existance, should have made me doubt, should have made me forget. Instead, her absence ached inside me.

I pulled into the parking lot on Chestnut Street in the late afternoon and went to the diner before I unpacked, aware that I was postponing climbing the stairs and searching out timid appeals for acknowlegement.

The September sunshine was warm as I walked back, but the buildings cast cold shadows through it. I passed back and forth from heat to chill, aware of the contrast and digging it. My senses were more alert than usual, and I loved the feeling, riding it like a high, registering sounds and smells and sensations, seeing the colors and the edges of things with a rare and joyous clarity.

My sight caressed the planters on either side of the Pythias doorstep—the purple pansies and red geraniums rising above the white and tan cigarette butts—then slid up the bricks to the stone lintel across the top of the door, read its carved letters, and stood and stared while I read it again:

Knights of Pythias

This building had a history. History is full of people. One of them might be a woman named Eleanor.

I sat on the curb and lit a cigarette. Butchie came out for a break and sat beside me.

"Beautiful day," he said, lifting his face to the sun.

"Yeah. Know anything about this building?"

He gave me one of his Looks—the one that said I had just bounced off the wall in an unexpected direction. Typically, he accepted the new tangent and considered my question. "No. . . .Well, yeah, a little. It was built in the 1800s—late 1800s, maybe? It was some sort

of store downstairs, and the Knights of Pythias Fraternal Order—kind of like the Masons, I think—built the second story on top of it and used it for a Lodge. The front part's been a shoe repair shop as long as I can remember, way before I bought it. I forget when the K of P moved out. Why?"

"Any pictures of it from way back when?"

"Ohhh," he said. "I get it. Pictures. No."

There wouldn't be any pictures of her, anyway.

I stubbed out my cigarette and went down the street to Butt Drugs, where I got a pint of vodka to put some kick in the Italian sodas and coffees I'd be drinking all evening.

Everybody at Pythias greeted me like I'd just come back from the dark side of the moon—except for the ones whose current self-image demanded pretending they hadn't noticed I was gone. They caught me up on local gossip; I told stories about my trip, some of which were true.

As the evening passed, I gradually withdrew from the general conversation. One or two people attracted me into exchanges, but I spent most of my time thinking and brooding, improvising on the guitar Butchie kept on hand.

I thought about a woman in a long dress. My knowledge of women's fashions was sketchy, but I would put the long skirt and shawl and piled-up hair I'd seen in my dream either before the 1920s or during the 1970s, and the camera I'd dreamed had definitely been late 1800s—cameras, I knew. So, a woman who lived around the time the place was built, a woman in a Fraternal Organization's lodgehouse, a woman who could barely print her own name, lonely and hungry for attention. Cleaning lady, I thought. I could see her, coming in after everybody else was gone, tidying up the remains of other people's comfortable companionship: emptying the ashtrays, throwing away the paper trash, dusting, sweeping, washing the dishes, turning out the lights, locking the door and leaving. Had she never been loved? Had she been loved and abandoned? Had she died young or middle-aged, or had she slogged through long thankless years? Had her life been empty of family and friends, or had it been full of them and only empty somewhere inside?

Still I kept myself from climbing the stairs. I wanted my homecoming to be solitary, with no other voices in the place but ours,

no other beings in the place but us.

The shop finally emptied. I locked up and did my cleaning by the just-sufficient illumination of the night security light. If I left the overhead light on, the patrons who lingered in the parking lot for an hour or more after closing would be knocking on the door wanting to come back in. Now, all the coffee and all the ashtrays were cold, and the only thing I wanted was to do my work and get my stuff out of the car and go upstairs to my home.

By the time I finished, the parking lot was empty. I stirred the trash cans one last time to be sure there weren't any hot ashes in with the paper, went out and loaded myself down with my suitcase and gear, locked up behind myself, and struggled up the stairs.

"I'm back. I told you I was coming back. Did you miss me?"

I felt a little stupid, talking to the empty rooms, but a little more *not* stupid. Eleanor—Elinir—was there, listening.

"I missed you," she said, tentatively.

"I missed, you, too. I'm glad to be back."

"Ah. . . ." The voice sounded surprised, gratified, satisfied, as if resting after a long labor. "Ah, Tom."

I had a sandwich and a cup of instant coffee and a shower, and grinned when I came out to find *Elinir* traced in the spilled coffee powder and sugar, right beneath where I had traced *Tom*.

It was past midnight, and I was suddenly very tired. The driving, the smoke—first-hand and second-hand, the vodka and the hour all hit me at once. I took off my shirt and fell into bed and dropped into a deep sleep.

"Tom!" Elinir's voice pushed into my consciousness.

My heart leapt toward it, ready to dream of her, ready to meet her in the dreamworld that lies outside of linear time.

She wasn't happy to see me, though. I could see her figure, but its brightness was muffled in heavy dark mist. Her hands were raised to ward me away.

"Tom! No! Wake up!"

"Wake up? Why? I just got here."

"Get out! Get out!"

I was shocked and hurt. "What did I do? Why, Elinir? What did I do?"

"You got to wake up, Tom! There's fire inside the walls! I can't do nothing to stop it—you got to wake up, Tom! Wake up and get out! Wake up!"

Her words didn't make sense. I was muddled and confused. The dark mist, I thought, must be smoke, but it didn't seem to be hard to breathe. In fact, I felt peaceful and light, and nothing was any trouble at all. Everything was fine. Happiness was within my grasp at last.

"I'll wake up in a minute," I said. I took a step forward. The brightness that was Elinir cleared and I saw her. She was as tall as I was, raw-boned and heavy-featured. She was what anybody but an artist would call plain, with a pock-marked complexion and thick, coarse black hair. She was beautiful—beautiful. I would never get tired of looking at her. She would never be a type, never look like anybody but herself, never lose her fascination.

She was crying, and I couldn't bear it. She raised her fists to her head and wailed, "Wake up! Please! Please!"

I took one more breath and the smoke blew away. I took Elinir in my arms and comforted her until her sobs quieted and she rested, calm, against my chest.

Together, we watched Pythias burn, watched our old lives turn to ash around us. I know in my head that my friends mourned my loss and I'm sorry for that, but I don't feel the loss, myself. I've passed outside time, where every instant is filled with love and joy, where nothing pulls me from my fulfillment, where Elinir and I roam the town by day and by night, in twilight and at dawn, where we're ever before each other's eyes, and her sweet voice calls, "Take my picture, Tom," and I do. And I do.

The Valiant Taste of Death
by
T. Lee Harris

Huey Scanlon couldn't believe his luck. He kept glancing in the rearview mirror of the rollback truck to reassure himself that the 1968 Plymouth Valiant was still there. It was. Every time. He settled back in the well-worn driver's seat and beamed into the snowflakes melting on the windshield.

Working at Woody's Gas Mart had a few perks. Being able to use the rollback car hauler any time he wanted was one; getting to read the *Bargain Mart* before anyone else was another. Bundles of magazines and newspapers were dropped off at the store in the early hours of morning and it was part of Huey's job to put them in their racks. They called his shift the graveyard shift for good reason: most nights it was plain *dead*. That made for plenty of time to leaf through the car listings. He'd found a lot of good deals for project cars that way, but the '68 was the best yet, so good he almost ripped the page circling it.

The listed price was sweet, too. A lot less than it should have been, but Scanlon lowballed it anyway just to see what would happen. Could have knocked him over with a feather when the guy took the offer without blinking. He should probably be ashamed, but hell! He worked at a gas station f'crissakes—it wasn't like he was rolling in cash, or anything. That was one of the reasons he bought fixer-uppers. It was fun restoring them and he usually made his money back and more when he sold them.

He frowned into the late winter flurry. It was strange, though. He got the impression the guy just wanted the Valiant gone. Couldn't figure why. She was a real beauty. Oh, sure she was a little rough in places and the upholstery was a wreck, but that was all part of restoring vintage cars. By spring, he'd have her in cherry condition and turn her around for a good profit. The reflective sign for his street caught his headlights through the snowy dusk. He turned onto the side road and bumped up his driveway. After that, the thought was forgotten in the busyness of getting the Valiant off the rollback and into the barn he'd converted into a workshop.

The rollback's motor sounded hollow amid the snow-covered trees lining the drive and flakes swirled through the big garage door as he gazed on his prize. Under the glare of the fluorescents, she looked angry. That would change. She was overdue for some TLC and he intended to spoon out a lot in the coming months—but not just yet. He glanced at his watch and winced. The snowfall wasn't heavy, but it slicked the roads enough to make the drive longer than he'd counted on. He and the rollback were due at the Gas Mart soon. He silently cursed Buddy Cottam for up and quitting the day before. That left them short-handed and both he and Woody having to pull extra shifts to cover. It meant extra money, which was good, but it also meant he was going to be busier than a one-armed paperhanger in a hurricane for a while. As much as he wanted to dive into it, the restoration would have to wait. He was always jazzed at the start of a new project and putting it on the back burner was going to be hard. He flipped off the light and hit the door close button. If he hurried, he'd have time to grab a burger before work.

His schedule kept him from doing anything like sanding or even popping the hood, but the auto parts place across from Woody's made it way easy to buy things. He laughed as he plopped the bulging bag onto the wooden workbench. One of his ex-girlfriends whined that if she was a car, he'd never have trouble buying a present for her. She was a bitch, but she had a point. At least he understood cars.

He upended the bag and sorted through the purchases. Setting the quarts of oil specially formulated for older engines aside, he turned his attention to the covers for the front bench seat. The old upholstery was torn and patched with every color tape imaginable. The rear seat was worse and there was nothing left of the headliner. None of that was a problem, though. He knew a couple of guys who ran an upholstery shop. Once the weather warmed up, he'd give them a call to see what sort of deal they could work out. She'd need paint, too. There was so much primer on her, it was hard to tell what her original color was.

There was movement in his peripheral vision, a silhouette of someone sitting in the driver's seat.

Huey whirled. "What the hell you doing—?" He stopped abruptly. The seat was empty.

"Damn, Scanlon! Now you're seeing things." Sagging against the workbench, he scrubbed at his eyes. If they didn't hire someone to replace Cottam soon, these double shifts were going to kill him.

He stretched and things popped. Man, he was looking forward to bed, but not before he gave the motor a good once-over and put the new seat covers on. The cell phone twittered. Flipping it open, he swore violently. Woody's Gas Mart. The past two days of snow had been topped off with a layer of ice. Someone probably needed towing. It was a pain, but that was the downside of being on call 24/7. He dragged a grubby pad of paper and pencil stub over and punched the answer button. "Speak, you're bein' spoke to."

"Hey, Huey," Woody graveled. "You up to makin' a run? Guy

skidded off the road out 337."

"Sure. I can handle it. Shoot me the info and I'll get right on it." He scribbled down name, tag number and directions, flipped the phone shut and gave in to a jaw-creaking yawn. So much for the once-over. His gaze fell on the leather steering wheel cover. At least he could get that on before he left.

Half-sitting in the car, he flicked the folds out of the thin leather and smoothed it along the top of the wheel. Yelping, he bounced back, blowing on fingers so cold they hurt. Damn, that thing was freezing. He'd have to fire up the heater before he did anything requiring manual dexterity. Seemed like nothing was going right on this project. Sighing, he tossed the leather cover onto the dashboard, slammed the door and hurried out.

It was three hours before Huey saw home again. Three *long* hours. The car that ran into the ditch on 337 had broken the rear axle. Before that one was even loaded onto the hauler, Woody called with another: a pickup wrapped itself around a tree out German Ridge Road. Getting the big rollback truck up his own driveway and onto the concrete parking pad wore him out as if he'd been physically pulling it rather than driving. He shut off the engine and flopped back in the seat, too tired to even get out of the cab. Summoning the will, he climbed out into the cold which went a ways to wake him up. He took one step toward the house and the beckoning bed, then stopped. No. He was going to get something done on that damned Valiant if it killed him.

The brightness of the overhead lights stabbed needles into his headache. Maybe it would be better to wait until he got some sleep. Then he saw the steering wheel cover lying on the floor a distance from the car. Oh man. If he needed more proof that he was tired, the fact he knocked something on the floor that he *thought* he'd left on the dash, was it. In neon. In flashing neon. Scooping the cover up, Scanlon tugged at the door handle. It didn't budge. It was locked. All the doors were locked. Add loopy to tired. He sure didn't remember locking one door let alone four.

Shaking his head, he dug the key out, scooted onto the driver's seat and put the cover on. There. One thing accomplished. Only a couple million more left to do.

Sunday rolled around again before he got a day off. It was great to sleep in and take his time over a pot of the special Hawaiian coffee and a couple magazines while he let the heaters in the workshop take the chill off. The weather had warmed a bit and the roads were cleared; the chances of being called out on a wrecker run were slim. He should have the whole day to work on the Valiant. Finally.

It was bright enough, he wouldn't even need the overhead lights. That was a nice change. When he entered through the small side door, a shaft of bright sunlight sliced across the floor illuminating something wadded up on the concrete. Puzzled, he went over and picked it up. It was the steering wheel cover. It was shredded and the lacings were nowhere to be seen. Was this someone's lame-brained idea of a practical joke? As he stared at the ruined leather, all the Valiant's door locks schunked down. Wheeling, he expected to see a kid or one of his friends jeering at him from inside. It looked empty. Anger rose. "Okay, whoever the hell you are! This ain't funny."

He ran around the car trying to glimpse someone inside, but there was seemingly no one and try as he might, he couldn't see the floorboard of the shadowed back seats.

Screaming obscenities, he snatched a tire iron from the bench, jammed the key in the passenger door lock and dived in part-way over the seat to slash the tool through the floor shadows. Nothing. No one. He sat back on his heels, panting and confused.

Slowly a hissing that had been just on the edge of his hearing became louder. Half-turning from where he knelt on the seat, he saw something like frost pouring out from where the hood met the windshield. The hiss grew louder as the frost spread across metal and glass, so cold it steamed. He leapt back, catching his foot on the rocker panel and landed hard. As he pulled himself up, mist oozed from under the front seat, tendrils reaching for him. He could feel the intense cold before they wrapped themselves around his throat and, impossibly, tightened. He fought against the hold, pushing with knees braced on the rocker. Blackness seeped around the edges of his vision as an angry face screaming words he couldn't hear formed in the mist before his eyes. Arms flailing, he brought the tire tool around with all his strength.

The tool hit nothing that he could tell, but when it passed

through, the mist vanished. The sudden release sent him sprawling on the oil-stained floor and the iron bounced away as he crab-crawled as fast as he could to put distance between himself and . . . whatever it was. He cowered against the far wall, gasping. As he watched, the car door slammed closed and the lock snapped down. Then, the frost melted away, appearing to flow back into the vehicle under the hood.

He fled.

Hands still shaking, Scanlon gulped a double shot of Jack Daniels then rested the glass against his forehead. What the hell just happened?

Had he seen a ghost? Ghosts weren't real! He didn't *believe* in ghosts. *Yeah, hot shot? Why not march right back out there, then?* One way or another, he was going to have to go back. He'd run out so fast, he'd left the side door open. Leaning against the edge of the kitchen sink, he watched the wooden door swing idly in the wind. The Valiant was clearly visible from where he stood. He nearly dropped the whiskey glass as a human figure solidified behind the wheel, then just as abruptly vanished.

Ooookay. He set the glass down carefully. Whether he believed in ghosts or not, something was happening. Maybe he was losing his mind, maybe there was something else. Whatever, it was time to hit the internet and do a little research on the previous owners.

It was a measure of how shaken he was that he entered his debit card information for the VIN report without so much as a grumble. The report wasn't very long and the list of past owners was even shorter. Two names. Thomas Bledsoe was the guy he bought the car from, so Vernon Bledsoe was probably his father. That fit with what he'd been told.

Entering Thomas' name in the various databases didn't yield much, just a few police reports of domestic disturbances. Vernon's name usually appeared in those, too.

Entering Vernon's name in the same databases generated page after page of police reports, arrest records, court documents and newspaper articles about fights and thefts. The arrest records and court documents were a shopping list of violence. It appeared, if there was any way to disturb the peace, Vernon Bledsoe had done it. Repeatedly.

At the end were the public notices of his death. Curiously antiseptic pieces that simply stated he had died around Thanksgiving the year before and that his son and daughter-in-law were his sole survivors.

Huey sat back staring at the screen and the many-times folded car title, nursing a warmed-over cup of coffee. Maybe he was missing something, but there didn't seem to be anything in all he'd read to explain what happened—other than Vernon Bledsoe, the Valiant's first owner, was a mean sunnovabitch. Maybe he'd call Tom and ask a few questions, although he had no idea what he'd actually ask. It didn't matter in the end. The recorded message he got said the number he had for Tom Bledsoe was no longer in service.

Resigned, he folded the car title and scribbled notes into his pocket. The pickup was gassed up, looked like a drive out to the Bledsoe place was in order. He had a bad feeling he knew what he'd find, though.

He hated being right. The Bledsoe house was empty and the garage stood open showing only a drift of snow inside. Slamming the truck door, he leaned against it, staring at nothing in particular, wondering what the hell to do next.

"You lookin' for the Bledsoes?" asked a woman's voice in back of him.

A thinnish middle-aged woman with curly graying hair stood at the end of the driveway across the road. She had her coat held closed against the cold wind with one hand and, in the other, held a lit cigarette.

He stepped around the pickup. "Yes, ma'am. Do you know how I can get ahold of them?"

She took a drag on the cigarette, held the smoke and considered him. Finally she said, "No sir, I wish I did. They up and skipped out on three months' rent one night a couple weeks back." She glared at the empty house and took another drag like she was sucking anger through the tobacco. Suddenly she shrugged. "Don't know what I'm mad about other than the cash lost. They was lousy renters and worse neighbors. I thought maybe it'd get better when the old man killed hisself, but it didn't."

Scanlon was surprised. "You mean Vernon? It was suicide?"

She waved dismissively. "Hell no. He didn't do it on purpose. The old bastard was too ornery to let everyone off that easy. It was an accident, sure enough."

He stared at the house. Empty windows stared back like sockets of a skull.

She looked at him sharply. "They owe you money, too?"

"Uhhh, no ma'am. I didn't know them that well. I bought a car off Tom and there's something needs clearing up on the papers." Not completely true, but it sounded good.

"Oh, you're the one bought old Vern's car? Not surprised Tom wanted to get shed of it. I think that damned Plymouth was the only thing Vernon Bledsoe really loved. In the end, that's what killed him."

Huey blinked.

She chuckled. "I see they didn't bother to tell you. Vernon died in it."

She waved toward the house, smoke trailing behind the gesture. "Tom and Darla moved in here a couple years back. They wasn't too bad then. Late with the rent a few times and a bit stand-offish, but not bad. A while after that—maybe a year—Vernon showed up. Said he needed a place to stay seein' as how he'd been tossed out of his boarding house. Found out later he was in jail.

"Anyways, Tom said he could stay until he found someplace else but they took to fighting almost as soon as he stepped in the house. Darla had enough and told him to shape up or get out. What he did was take over the garage and live outta that car. Wasn't too bad in summer, but winter hit hard and early. That garage never was heated, so Vern would run the Plymouth for a spell to warm it up of a night."

Scanlon suddenly understood. "And one night, he fell asleep before he shut the car off."

She nodded and blew a jet of smoke at the open garage. "Hateful old man. Probably hauntin' the place now."

"I don't think you have to worry about that," he said. He thanked her and got back in the truck. She was still staring after him as he put it in gear and headed home.

It took a couple days for him to venture back out to the workshop. When he did, Vernon Bledsoe was waiting for him. The old man sat gripping the wheel with both hands, glaring hate as Scanlon entered. He was sort of see-through, going almost solid, then phasing away to a misty shape, then solid again. Huey leaned against the jamb, watching

for several minutes. "Okay," he said at last. "I believe in ghosts, now. You happy?"

Although there was no reply, he had the distinct impression the answer was no. He walked around the Valiant, keeping his tone conversational. "I been thinking about it and I really don't see your problem, Vern. From what I hear, you loved this car and all I'm wanting to do is fix her up."

The half-transparent figure didn't move, but Huey knew he was being watched. It felt creepy. He drew even with the driver's side window and stopped. "Now, are you going to work with me on this?"

Suddenly, the ghost of Vernon Bledsoe filled the window, fists waving, face contorted with fury, obviously screaming, but making no sound. Huey leapt back in sudden terror, then blinked, took a deep breath and got his racing heart under control. "I'm sorry you feel that way, Vern. Sorry but not surprised." Without another word, he turned and went back into the house. The last sight he had was of Vernon Bledsoe making an obscene gesture.

Morning dawned cold and clear as Scanlon backed the truck up to the steep stretch of riverbank. He'd driven quite a distance to find just the right spot: Secluded, deep and fast-running.

Backing up to the very brink of the steep bank, he got out and went around to unhook the securing chains hooked onto the axle. At his touch, frost spread and bitter cold seeped through his gloves. "Might as well give that a rest, Vern. You ain't even slowing me down."

Chains well out of the way, he straightened and rested his hand on the control levers for a moment. He really regretted what he was going to do. She was a great car, but. . . . He slammed the lever back and the truck's hydraulics growled into life, raising the front of the hauler until the Valiant rolled back off the flat bed. There was a huge splash as she hit the water. Huey walked over and looked down. The Valiant was floating out into the snow-melt flooded river, but taking on water quickly. The ghost of Vernon Bledsoe pounded a transparent fist on the window and shouted silent obscenities at him. He called out, "What's your problem, Vern? Once you hit bottom, ain't nobody gonna bother you and that car again. Bon voyage, asshole!"

Water boiled, then the thickly flowing current closed over it

like smooth hot chocolate. Huey watched the spot for a while longer, then put the bed level again. He started to swing up into the cab, then paused. Walking back to the embankment, he dug the ring of keys out of his pocket and flung them as hard as he could at the water. They arced out, glinting in the strengthening sunlight, then vanished in the muddy flow. He dusted his hands at a job well finished.

There was a diner a few miles back toward town. A cup of coffee and a plate of eggs sounded awful good right about now.

The Haunted House

by

Teddi Robinson

My middle child, Tom, yelled, "Mom! Dad! Grandma! Somebody come here, there's a man sitting on the foot of my bed! Mom, please!"

"You know there isn't anyone in the house except us. You don't want to go to sleep," my husband Dan answered.

"Please, Mom come here. He's grinning."

"Tom, if I come in there, I'm going to spank you. Now go to sleep!" Dan replied.

My mother-in-law said, "If Tom said he saw a man, then he saw a man, and you are not going to spank him . . . unless you spank me, too."

During the conversation, I had gone to Tom's bedroom. I didn't see anything, but I did take Tommy in my arms to comfort him until he was quiet and went to sleep.

We moved to this apartment because Dan lost his job. The apartment was part of a one-family home. After the owner passed away, they converted the house into a duplex. One side was three rooms and a large sun porch overlooking the river. Our side had three rooms and a small porch. The bathroom sat between the two kitchens with a hall in front and was shared by both families. It was what we could afford, since I wasn't working. Our third child was due any time and we completed the move just a couple of days before Ray was born. The two older children stayed with my mother-in-law while I was in the hospital, and this was our first time back.

With the children settled in bed, Dan took his mother home and I was left alone . . . I thought?

I was reading and thought I heard someone talking. I checked the children's room and looked out the kitchen door. Nothing and nobody. Maybe Carol, the girl next door, had her radio or TV on. I went to the door on my side of the connecting hallway and knocked.

"I was wondering, Carol, do you have your radio or TV on?" I asked.

"No, I don't. Why?"

After I related the evening events, Carol said, "I'll come over and stay with you and the kids till your husband gets back."

I said, "Thanks, I'd like that." Carol didn't know how relieved I was.

A few nights later, I was reading on the couch which was placed in front of the pocket doors separating our living room from Carol's. I heard Dan in the kitchen and kept on reading. I felt an arm go around my shoulders. Not bothering to look up, I just assumed it was Dan. He was proud of the fact that he could move without being heard.

"Hey, Thea, would you like some tea?" Dan asked from the other room.

"Weren't you here, beside me?" I asked.

"I'm in the kitchen, why?"

"Oh, come on now," I scoffed. "Weren't you just in here and put your arm around me?"

"I'm telling you, I haven't left the kitchen. Why?"

"I just felt an arm go around my shoulders and thought it was you." I shivered. "The other night when you took Mom home, I heard a couple of people talking. I couldn't hear what they were saying but they were talking."

"I think you and Tom have over-active imaginations."

"Maybe, you're right, but I don't think so."

Carol knocked and I let her in.

"Did you all drop something?" Carol asked.

"No, why?" I answered.

"There was this loud sound like someone dropping a large trunk or piece of furniture."

"Sorry, Carol," I said with a laugh. "It isn't time for me to move furniture . . . yet."

A couple of nights later, I awoke in the middle of the night to find a short, bald-headed, heavyset man standing at the foot of the bed. He grinned a toothless smile.

I went back to work and took the children to Mrs. Brown, the babysitter.

When Dan and I went to pick up the children, I decided to tell Mrs. Brown about our experiences. Mrs. Brown was a very good listener and supplied insight.

She said, "You just described Mr. Tyant. He was bedridden for years. They said he committed suicide in the bathroom."

I became very excited because I knew where he committed suicide and exactly how.

I didn't know how I knew these things, but I said, "He hung himself on a pink wall fixture in the bathroom. The wall fixture was too high for him to reach, so he dragged a chair to the wall, climbed on it, and put the rope around the light fixture and his neck. Then he kicked the chair away. The thing I don't understand is, if he was bedridden, how did he do this by himself?"

"I've wondered that myself a lot," Mrs. Brown replied. "That was the official ruling. Death by suicide."

Dan asked, "Thea, how do you know this?"

"It's just my woman's intuition, but if you look behind the door that is stored in the hallway, you will find the light fixture," I answered.

When we returned home, Dan rushed to the hallway. Just as I had said, the light fixture was behind the stored door in the hall between the two kitchens.

We didn't stay that night or any other night in that house, but moved in with my mother-in-law until we found another place to live.

Haunted
by
Marian Allen

My grandmother's living shadow drifts . . .

into the living room,
settles by the table of
crosswords and pencils
waiting and idle . . .
past the sewing room
stacked with folded cloth,
unaltered alterations,
patterns of the past . . .
through the kitchen,
appetite and laughter
almost plucking at her,
leaving her untouched . . .

Lord, the spirit is willing
but the chain of flesh is strong.
How she longs to break that chain,
to die, and then—to dance!

originally appeared in Serendipity Sampler by
Serendipity Systems electronic publishing.

Grady Gets His

by
Ginny Fleming

Have you ever seen something that's not there? Have you ever *not* seen something that *was* there? An invisible ghost is a little harder to see than your usual garden variety spirit.

Case in point: Recently, in Corydon, at a gathering of friends in a house on Mulberry Street, my husband and I joined in the fun of an outdoor card game. It was an enjoyable day, the eats were phenomenal, and friends were catching up on each other's lives, reconnecting after the long Southern Indiana winter. My husband was more into the card game than I, and I was wilting in the heat, so I retired into the house to relax under the cool of the ceiling fan.

Sipping an icy beer, I noticed my friend's mild-natured cat playing at my feet. Calling, I coaxed her up into my lap for a few ear scratches. "Dottie," I whispered, "you're such a sweetie! Becky's so lucky to have you." Though she seemed to be enjoying the attention, I wondered why she wasn't purring. Then I remembered. Dottie was a little backward. She didn't know how to "talk" didn't ever utter more than a squeek. But, her disability seemed to just make her sweeter.

Not so, Grady, Becky and Roger's outside cat who lived in their yard-side shop. "Sweet" never was a word used about Grady. He was a tom, with everything and every attitude that entails and on this special day, he'd been allowed into the house.

I knew Grady'd had a history of terrorizing Dottie. So, when he appeared from out of a side room and sauntered lazily toward us, it was no surprise my mild-mannered furry friend leaped from my lap to take cover under the sofa. Grady took this to mean the battle was on.

"Grady," I bluffed, "mind your manners, bud. I'll put your butt out the door just like Becky would. You better treat Dottie right." Bluffing was *just* what I was doing. I had no craving to be savagely razored by a bully-tom who was on his own rightful turf, so I made to go to the back door to call for my friend.

Dottie chose that moment to leave the safety of her hiding place, and Grady pounced. Thankfully, it was a light tussle and Dottie

scampered away from her tormentor pretty much unscathed. Grady growled and stalked after sweet Dottie.

Suddenly, something lifted Grady up from the floor and flipped him, snarling and cussing, onto his back where it roughed up the beefy tom for a good fifteen seconds more. By the time he'd escaped the invisible clutches of his invisible foe, Grady was good and mad. With much disgruntled yowling, Grady stormed to the back door and the safety of the backyard. Dottie was safe.

I looked at the sweet cat, serenely resting under a living room table. She seemed to be smiling.

After I rejoined my friends in the backyard, I found Becky and recounted "Grady's Big Battle". She appeared unimpressed. "Oh. That's just the ghost," she said. "He seems to like Dottie. Doesn't think a whole lot of Grady, though."

Out of Respect
by
Bonnie L. Abraham

They are all dead now, I thought, when I read the obituary. *Every one of the Demon Dozen is dead. Marshall was the last.* I folded the paper and laid it on the table beside my plate, and wondered what I should do. Pop would expect me to go to the funeral, but I wouldn't know anyone there, and they wouldn't know me. Still—Pop would expect it of me. I wasn't sure why the expectations of a man who had been dead for fifteen years mattered, but they did. And it wasn't like the funeral was a long distance away. Marshall's family lived in the county and the body was at Beanblossom's. I could walk there. Not that I would. There would be a graveside service, too.

I drank my now-cold coffee and went upstairs for my shower. I dressed in my navy suit. *Respectful.* No flashy jewelry, I told myself. It was only ten, and the funeral wasn't until one. I decided to have lunch at Joy'z, but it was still too early, even for that, so I grabbed the book I was reading and headed for the porch swing.

As I expected, Pop was already there, dressed in his too-tight grey suit. It was the only one he had, and he refused to get another, in spite of the fact that he was in danger of firing a button at someone's head with his next breath.

"At least unbutton the jacket," I told him.

"Can't. The pants won't button."

I sat on the swing beside him and opened my book.

"Thanks for this," he said.

"No problem," I said.

We sat in silence. I finished the book and checked my watch. Time for lunch, if I didn't want to be rushed for the funeral. Pop was gone again, so I went to Joy'z by myself. He would probably be along later.

I ordered my standard club sandwich and iced tea. Karen, the waitress, asked if Pop was along. I could see the relief on her face when I said he wasn't. He had been known to cause trouble at times. He remembered the place as Jocko's when his antics were appreciated

by a less refined clientele. It was sometimes embarrassing, but what's a person to do? If he wanted to come, I sure couldn't stop him!

I ate my lunch and checked my watch again. It was time. I paid the bill, left a tip on the table and drove to the funeral home. There weren't many people. I figured the woman sitting in front by herself was Marshall's wife. I went up and introduced myself, gave her my condolences and then went to the casket. Pop joined me.

"Don't look like I remember him," said Pop.

I nodded. He didn't look like the person I had seen, although I could see it was the same man—or someone who looked like his father might have looked. We took seats toward the back. As it turned out, we could have sat closer; there were plenty of empty chairs.

"You'd think some of the others would have come," said Pop.

What could I say? I knew why they hadn't; they were all dead.

"Well, their families could have come," said Pop, as though he read my thoughts. "Out of respect."

The funeral was short. It was obvious the minister hadn't known Marshall or anything about the Demon Dozen. That saddened Pop—me, too, for that matter. Marshall's widow should have said something. Then again, maybe she didn't know, either. They had been a tight-lipped group. If they hadn't held their reunions at our house until Pop died, I probably wouldn't have known about them either. Even at that, I didn't know what they had done, only that they existed. It had been understood when they came for the reunions that no one spoke of their time together in the Marines until I had left. I don't know if they spoke of it after I left or not, but somehow, I doubted they did. All Pop had told me was that it had been a terrible time.

Ours was the only car besides the widow's and the hearse to go to the graveside. It was a beautiful spring day and there were flowers in bloom everywhere. A good thing, since there was only the spray of roses on the casket. The minister read a passage from the Bible, prayed and dismissed us. I paid my respects to the widow. Pop went to the casket and saluted.

"Did you see them?" said Pop, after we got into the car.

"See who?" I asked.

"We were all there. The Dozen."

We were silent on the rest of the short drive home. "You're a good daughter," said Pop, as we pulled into the driveway. I turned to thank him, but he was gone.

A Little Ditty Bout Jack & Diane
by
Ginny Fleming

Another night. Home alone . . . in this big rambling house on Corydon's North Capitol Avenue. Seems like forever I've been alone. Ever since my "Angel" realized the culmination of her labors. . . . yeah. She really put her heart and soul into it, thought it out, down to the tiniest detail.

First, she told everyone at my high-school reunion I was losing my memory. My reaction? I chuckled. Doesn't everyone have their senior moments? After we returned home, and I mentioned it to her, told her it hurt me a little, she apologized. Then, as a kind of peace offering, she brought me a cup of that new nut tea she'd found at the Tea Cottage. Good tea. I'd had three cups a day, like clock-work, for the past month. Morning, noon and right before bed.

Next, she changed her cooking pattern to a more spicy Tex-Mex menu. I liked it, even though it played hell with my stomach, and I missed her old country cooking. Pretty soon, my belly was giving me fits. No matter what I ate, like as not, I was in for a late night of indigestion. But, Diane . . . my Angel never seemed bothered and she always had the same things on *her* plate. I mentioned it, but she claimed there was a wicked bug going around. I must'a caught something, she said. I chugged buckets of Pepto and let it go.

Then, there were the cigarettes. Cancer sticks. One after another. No, not *me*, her. Some nights, you'd'a thought she was a house on fire. When I told her *sweetly* I was worried for *her* health, she sneered "You'll go *way* 'fore me, Sweetcheeks". My Angel . . . always the concerned one. Didn't want me to grieve. Then, to lighten the mood, she blew smoke in my face . . . I choked and coughed . . . she laughed . . . we both laughed. Diane . . . what a kidder.

Finally, the day came when I couldn't deny the pain. The doctor said it was too late. Gave me months instead of years, and I could tell he was "fluffing up" about the months part. I was crushed, depressed and angry, naturally. Why did God do this to me? *Why?*

Diane? She put on a brave face. I never saw her cry. Not once. My Angel. She refused to discuss my impending . . . impending . . . I

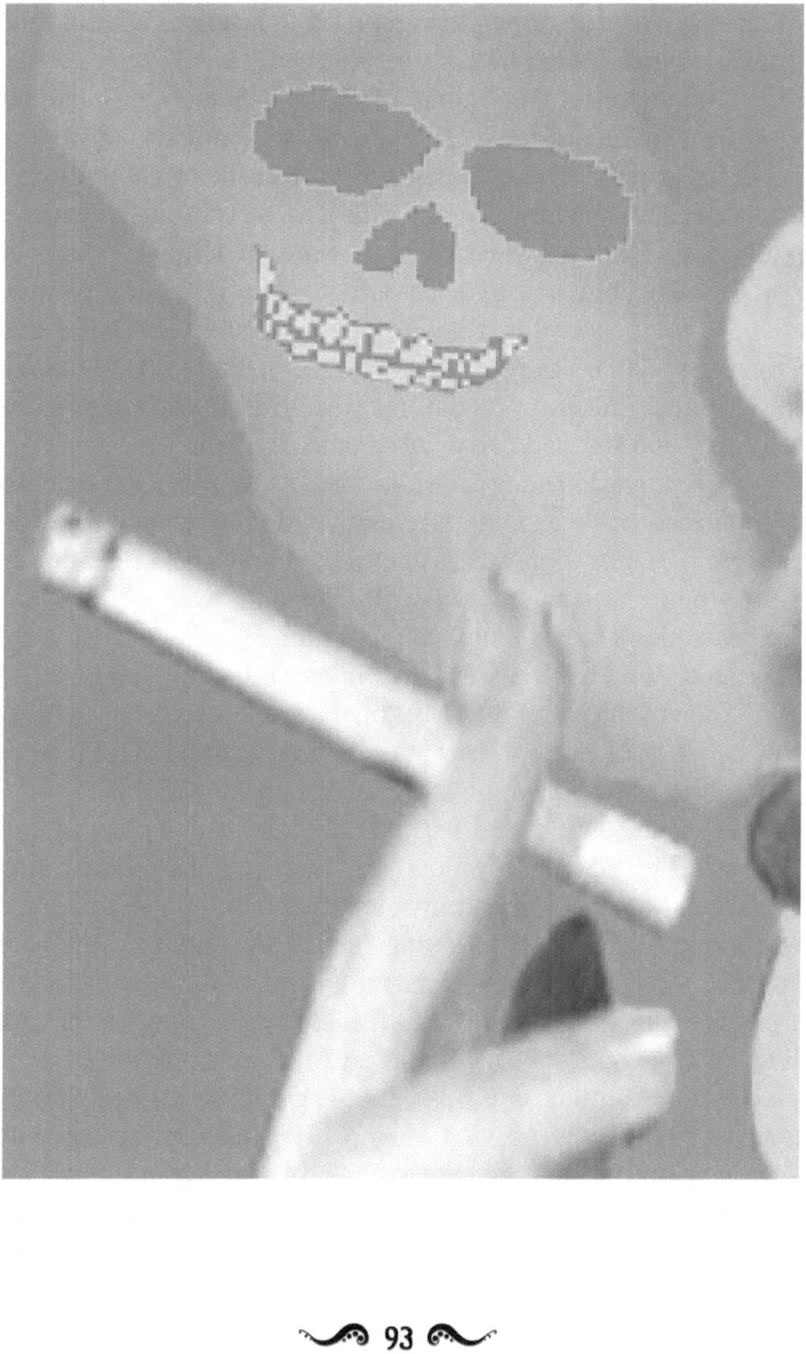

couldn't even say the word. Diane just chuckled and made a joke about it. Called it my "big farewell party". Ahh . . . my Angel. The things she did to keep my spirits up. Like the time she tied me to an arm chair. Told me she was just helping me get used to hospice. What a card. I still snicker when I think of that one. Ahhh. . . .

. . . memories. Good times. There was one time, she told my sister I wasn't taking visitors. God bless my sis. Hardheaded Wendy— that was my childhood nickname for her—barrelled right through the front door and found her way to my bedroom. Saw through my Angel's playful prank. Oh, the giggles filled the house *that* night.

I finally got Diane to discuss my upcoming . . . death—there I said it. At first, she wanted nothing of "the talk". But, after much coaxing, she relented and we talked into the night. I told her I thought a simple military funeral would be nice, as I'd spent many happy years in the Army and she said one word to that: Cremation.

My expression must have clued her. I was, frankly . . . shocked. She spluttered her reasoning and explanation. Cremation was less expensive . . . Cremation was easier on the family . . . Cremation was greener—better for the environment. Cremation would be easier on *her*. She wouldn't have to think of me rotting . . . all alone in the cold, cold ground. My Angel. Always and forever thinking of me.

Then the big day came. My "big farewell party". Diane begged her preacher to officiate . . . to put me in the ground. That's when I began putting two and two together.

I was standing by the urn, my Army photo in a place of honor in front of it. I gazed out at my mourners. There was Hardheaded Wendy in the second row. Diane and my step-kids took up the whole front row. I smiled. My blended, loving family was gathered to bid me farewell. Surely, I was a blessed man. Surely, I was a *loved* man. Then, the preacher—I *supposed* he was the preacher—stepped up to the podium, and announced to my family and friends: "Jack wasn't always a *good* man . . . until he was saved by the goodness of love—until he was saved by the love of a *good* woman." He ended that sentence with a knowing glance and a wink sent to my . . . Angel. My grieving Angel.

My eyes shot to Wendy's face, and for one fleeting moment I truly thought my Angel would be joining me prematurely. Like I said . . . two and two adds up pretty slowly. If you're me.

I returned home and sat down in front of the huge screen television that I didn't know we needed until Diane drug it home . . . the month before my . . . "party". It took me a few minutes to turn it on, but I finally mastered the trick. It's pretty simple, really. Just gotta think more. In fact, it's kind of a *mind-push* than a physical thing. Anyhow, there I was watching some strange show that had a lot of clouds and some too-precious music like some New-Age-Yanni stuff. About the time I was ready to change the channel, Diane walked in the door, followed by the preacher, and the channel changed to the local news. On its own. I didn't have to push or anything.

I almost called out to my Angel, wanting to welcome her home. Then I remembered she had a guest . . . and I was dead. Instead I chuckled, shook my head, and sat back on the sofa, new in fact, same as with the television . . . and . . . many other things since my . . . "party".

Silly me. Here I was feeling sorry for my grieving Angel. Here I was mentally thanking the preacherman for consoling the new widow. Here I was . . . then I watched him take Diane into his arms and lay one on the love of my life like I hadn't been able to do for months . . . a lifetime ago. All the pieces came together in a rush, and suddenly, I was *very* thankful I finally figured out how to turn on that big screen television.

I think, with enough practice, I'll be able to switch the labels from a certain nut tea to the vanilla flavor my Angel prefers. Hopefully, Preacherman likes *his* tea on the nutty side, too.

Midnight Clear
by
Marian Allen

Hollis Lanthorn died at Christmas—got tanked up on spiked cider and took his school bus out on the back roads for a late-night spin. Everybody said it was God's mercy he didn't hit anyone, what with all the people out for Midnight Mass, but it happened that Holly went over the bluff and up in flames all by himself. He had been the crabbiest driver in the system, he was divorced and childless, and all his family had "preceded him in death", as the paper put it, so the school bus was generally considered more of a loss than Holly.

Kids said he was damned for driving drunk on Christmas Eve and that, on frosty winter nights, he drove a bus with red headlights along his old route. It was Kevin Ferdusi, age eleven, who concocted that story. Nobody could have been more surprised than he was ten years later, when he saw the ghost bus, himself.

Kevin, now 21, had been to a Christmas Eve party. He hadn't been invited, but he had heard the music from his trailer so he'd wandered down the road and nobody threw him out. Next thing he knew, it was two in the freezing morning and he was staggering along the verge trying to pronounce "Wenceslaus" without spitting or dribbling.

The radio's prediction of "patchy, dense fog in low-lying areas" had never been more accurate. The party had been on a ridge and his trailer was on a ridge, but the road between them ran down through a hollow, and now the world was lost in swirls of mist like cold, damp angel-hair.

The sound of a motor penetrated the fog in his brain, and lights—red lights—lit up the fog around him.

"Yo, Rudolph," he said, and stepped further onto the gravel shoulder.

But it wasn't Rudolph, it was a school bus with red headlights. It stopped next to him, and the door creaked open, sending out a familiar burst of muggy air filled with the smells of over-heated bodies and, weirdly, evergreens and peppermint. He looked at the driver and almost

took another step back, into the ditch.

Holly was bloated and pasty-faced, with limp black hair cut short on the sides and combed over a bald spot on the top, a ratty mustache like a dead caterpillar above his upper lip and black-and-gray stubble on his cheeks. In other words, he looked just as he had in life.

Kevin glanced down at the bus steps. Yes, they were stained with brown ice. Even as he saw this, a jet spurted from Holly's mouth onto the gravel at Kevin's feet, leaving a trail of droplets to steam and freeze on the risers.

"You gonna stand there like a idiot, or you gonna get on the bus?"

Kevin thought about that.

Holly made the doors waggle. "Get on the bus, Ferdusi!"

Kevin got on, avoiding the tobacco slick out of remembered habit.

The doors hissed shut behind him.

Before anything else, he noticed the decorations. Dried-out evergreen wreaths with gummy-looking candy canes tied to them hung in some of the windows, and bedraggled red bows were tied around the hand-grips on the ends of the seats. They looked like—he realized they probably were—leftovers from a previous Christmas, picked up after they had been thrown away. Then he saw that he and Holly were not alone. There were fifteen passengers scattered throughout the bus, some in twos and threes, but most were alone. Some of them, he had known pretty well. Some he had known only to speak to or by sight, and a couple he didn't recognize. The ones he knew, he hadn't seen for a while. He had been to a couple of the funerals.

"So, you dead, boy?" Holly grunted.

"Dead drunk." It didn't seem like that ought to count. Kevin had a vague feeling of ill-use.

"I gotta let you off, then. You still live in that trailer, top of the hill?"

Relieved, Kevin nodded. Between the close call and the heat, he was sweating. He took off his black leather jacket.

His dad was a tattoo artist, and had freebee'd Kevin as soon as the boy turned eighteen. Dad had moved to Chicago, where business

was better and more demanding, but he had left a testament to his ability. From wrist to ankle, foot to chin, Kevin bore tattoos of creatures real and fantastic, symbols of every faith, and people of all nations, times, forms, and states of dress or undress. The arms and neck Kevin bared when he shed his jacket were covered with pattern and color. And, tonight, they glowed.

First softly, then brighter, the colors shimmered and twinkled. It didn't hurt. Kevin couldn't feel it happening at all, except as a thrill deep inside, a thrill that grew deeper and stronger at the delight on his fellow passengers' faces.

"Well, well, well," Holly rumbled. "Whaddya know about that?"

Kevin was sorry his ride would be over soon. Any minute, the bus would start up the hill and out of the fog. It would happen any minute. Any minute, now.

It didn't happen. It kept on not happening.

Cool!

Happily, he walked further into the bus and grabbed a hand-strap on either side of the aisle.

He took a deep breath of warm air and sang as much as he could remember of "Deck the Halls". Before he ran out of memory, others had joined in, and most of the words got filled in by somebody or other. After a couple more carols, accompanied by the merry winking lights of Kevin's tattoos, the scattered passengers had moved into seats close to him and were roaring songs in good cheer. Every so often, Holly would crank the doors open, letting in a blast of fresh, cold air and sending out a stream of tobacco juice.

After a while, Kevin sat down. The guys he knew introduced him to the folks he didn't know, and he caught everybody up on town gossip.

Holly's gravel voice broke through laughter. "Sun's about to come up. Time I dropped you off home, Ferdusi."

The passengers groaned.

"This was the best Christmas since I got on this bus."

"This was my best Christmas ever!"

"Hey, Ferdusi, think you could come back next year?"

"Maybe he can make it sooner."

"Get real!"

Kevin stood and picked up his jacket. "You only make this run on Christmas or what?"

Holly shrugged. "Sometimes we're making the run and there's Christmas lights, sometimes there's not."

"Hey—" one of his new acquaintances said, "maybe you'll be riding with us all the time, some day."

Holly and the other passengers protested the idea, drowning out Kevin's breathless, "Thanks a lot—PAL!"

"Nah, look at 'im!" An old guy, formerly janitor at the Uptown Cinema, cocked a thumb at Kevin's body art. "Whadda you think— Does he go in or not?"

"In. In!" the other passengers shouted, and the kid who had made the suggestion conceded, waving his hands in the air.

The fog outside the bus windows had taken on a silver gleam. The bus started up the hill toward the far ridge.

Kevin grabbed the handholds again. "In where? What are you talking about?"

The passengers looked at each other, uncomfortable and shame-faced.

"Paradise," Holly grunted over his shoulder.

"Yeah," said the janitor. "We go up there every so often and look through the gate. It's freakin' beautiful!"

Kevin heard murmurs, saw nods, and felt the longing that filled the bus.

"They won't let you in? Like, Saint Peter is guarding the gate and he keeps you out?"

"Guy out front with a sword," said Holly. "Don't know his name. He spots us, puts down the sword and starts waving to us. Waving us in, see?"

The incline the bus climbed increased a couple of degrees.

Kevin looked from Holly to the others. "So he's waving you in – Why don't you go in?"

One of Kevin's old pals gave him a "don't be stupid" glare.

"He can't see us in the bus. If he did, he'd slam the gate in our face. Drunks, druggies, suicides, whatever. We ended up here because we don't deserve better. We know that."

The passengers grew grayer as the fog outside lightened.

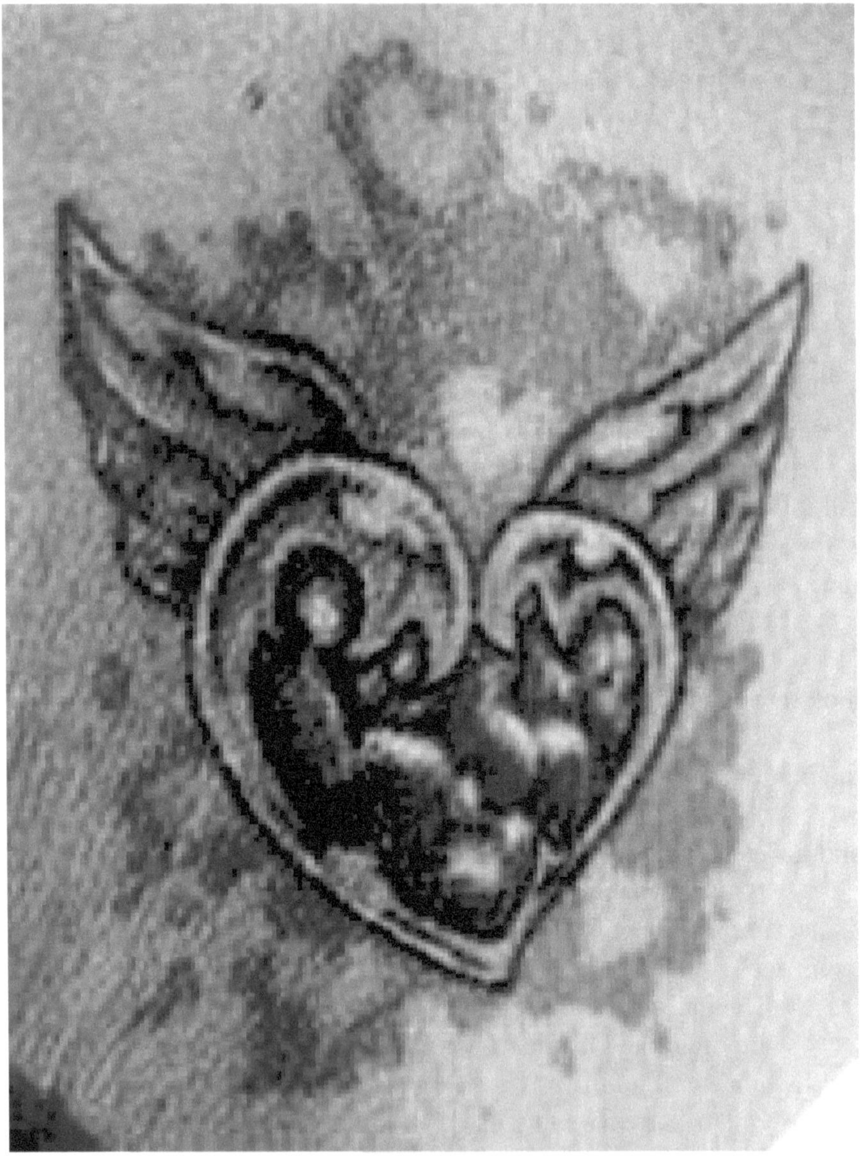

"But look at *you*." A middle-aged woman who kept her wrists tucked against her waist smiled at him with a purity of joy that hurt him to see. "They'll *have* to let *you* in."

Kevin touched a glittering dragon. "Because of these?"

"Yeahhhh."

He knew what they meant. When Dad had told him, "Mom tried to get better, but she was just too sick," he had understood. Mom died because he, Kevin, wasn't worth living for. That certainty had lasted until he turned eighteen, when Dad's present had been any tattoo he wanted. Kevin's choice had been a five-color collar of flowers, leaves and vines. Including the black outline, that had meant six long sessions, with time to heal in between. At first, it had hurt like hell. It had hurt as much as he deserved to hurt, a worthless guy like him. But all the time Dad worked, he had talked. Talked about Kevin: Kevin in Mom's belly, Kevin in Mom's arms, Kevin in Mom's heart, and in Dad's. "Funny talking to you about you," Dad had said. "I talk about you all the time when I'm working, I kinda forgot it was you I was talking to." After that, the tattoos didn't hurt so much. After that, they weren't made out of pain and blood, but out of beauty and love—gifts he and his father gave each other.

The dragon moved beneath his finger. Kevin looked at it. He pressed it. It curled and buckled, as if it were a painted transparency on the surface of his skin. He pinched the edge between the nails of his thumb and forefinger and peeled it, painlessly, away.

The bus was silent as he bent over and smoothed the dragon onto the janitor's forearm. The old man blinked, then vanished.

Hope washed through the bus, but nobody said a word. Nobody looked at Kevin, although he could feel the want coming off them in waves.

He plucked a rose and transferred it to the scarred wrist of the middle-aged woman. A tiger for one old pal, an ankh for another. A flaming sword, a Celtic knot, a Spanish dancer....

His arms were bare. The bus was empty except for himself and Holly.

They stopped and the doors squealed open. Kevin eased into his jacket, avoiding Holly's eyes.

"Go on, get off the bus, Ferdusi. It ain't gettin' no warmer out

there."

Kevin reached up. He fumbled a little, but at last he found the end and unfastened the collar of flowers, vines, and leaves, his first tattoo. It glittered as if it were the light and the facets that caught the light, both at the same time.

Holly glared at it, but he kept his hands on the wheel. The driver's neck was enormous, but the radiance expanded to encircle his throat.

"Thanks for the ride, man," Kevin said, and found he was talking to himself, standing at the mouth of his driveway, watching the sun come up.

Harboring Ghosts
by
J. Baumgartle

I choose my ghosts carefully,
predisposed as I am to have one,
my spiritual perceptions residing
in a restless corridor between
physical reality and dreams.

Departed loved ones and friends
come to me chatting pleasantly,
arrange and rearrange the guilt flowers,
always on my table
in a vase of forgiveness;

Ignore my absent responses
as in an agony of preconception
hypothesized from writings,
I welcome unmet authors, poets,
and other students of truth—

Cry out at the discovery
of pieces of myself —each
composer or performing artist
whom I would recognize even
soundlessly, in the dark. . . .

Other less desirable pasts
and presents and futures are
ill-at-ease in this markedly
vocal assembly—go elsewhere,
hoping for likelier midnights.

Buffalo Trace
By
Ardis Moonlight

The headlights on the Indiana patrol car bounced off the white blanket of air. Clyde hated nights like this—the fog so thick you could probably spoon it and taste the damp curls—a typical early spring night on the stretch between Corydon and Georgetown. Clyde checked the speedometer and eased off the accelerator. His fingers clutched the wheel, ready.

Deer frequently leapt through the mist, a cow and its calf might wander across the lanes, or a motorcyclist could lie sprawled in the wide median, the cycle still spinning. And sometimes the night was just quiet fog—those were the ones he liked.

Clyde glanced at the time on the dashboard—3:30 a.m.—then took a sip of hot coffee. Just a few more hours, and he'd be home. He pulled off the interstate, turned off the motor and listened to the quiet. He heard the swish of a car across the median heading west. When he looked ahead to the right, he noticed tire tracks leading through the muddy verge, but couldn't spot a vehicle. *Shit!*

He got out of the car and walked to the edge, listening to his breath and the sound of his boots crunching through the gravel, mud and grass. Clyde shined the flashlight along the ground—the tracks disappeared where the land sloped. He tried to remember how steep it was, and then stepped into the thick silence. At the bottom of the small hill, the flashlight caught glimmering bits, which looked like metal.

As he walked toward the glitter, Clyde felt he was being watched. He glanced around, but didn't see anything except fog. Occasionally a soft snort whispered through the white. *Probably deer.*

Clyde reached the mass of metal, knelt and examined the mangled glass, leather, steel, and plastic. He picked up the hood figure—the Mercedes symbol. Good Lord, he thought, what caused this—it looked as if a truck had run over it. He walked carefully around the car's remains, but didn't spot any blood.

Moving slowly to the left of the car and away from the road, Clyde glided the light through the heavily trampled tall grasses. *Cows?* He almost stepped on the dark mass just below his foot. *God, the stench*

and the mess! Holding his nose, he played the light over the pieces of a body—everything was crushed. He had seen something similar when someone decided suicide was the solution on the railroad track.

He looked at the trampled grasses again and noticed the prints— *so many of them*—that gouged out the clay soil.

The louder snorting caught his attention. Clyde warily glanced around, listening hard. The feeling of being watched was so strong, he felt all the hairs on his neck and back come to attention. He ran as fast as he could up the slope to the car, pulled open the door, got in quickly, and slammed and locked the door. *What the hell happened here?* Clyde reached for the car phone.

Sue Beth couldn't remember when she first started loving buffalo. Maybe when she was a kid, and the family had taken a vacation in South Dakota, and had watched the big, burly animals at home on the prairie. She had been entranced.

When the white buffalo calf had been born several years ago in Wisconsin, she had made a special trip to see it, and had been deeply moved by the experience.

Finishing college, finding a job, and then marrying had put any thoughts about buffalo out of mind for ten years or more. Lately, however, she had been imagining them as she made the trip from New Albany to Corydon, where she worked several days a week. Driving along the interstate, she could picture enormous herds running across the highway, through the pastures and up along the rolling hills. *What a sight—cars and trucks would skid everywhere!*

The job and being alone in the car were her avenues of sanity. Marriage had changed her, she knew. She wanted to leave but was afraid of what her husband might do.

It hadn't been that way at first. When she met John Cuff McDuff, the only child of too-old parents, his thick, red beard had been the chief draw. He had looked so much like the TV actor Sebastian Cabot. She had thought John would be like that—kind, gentle, loving and compassionate.

Two weeks after they married, he had shaved the beard because his mother had hated it. The smooth face was so bare and so unfamiliar; Sue Beth felt she had married someone else. With the beard loss came

a sharp-edged husband who trampled everything she did, telling her that the beliefs and ideas she had were "a waste of time and stupid."

At first she had argued with him, but that had ceased with his yelling and cursing. Once, he had grabbed her arm and pushed her to the floor, towering above and saying, "I'll tame you like any wild horse." She had cried, feeling like a prisoner.

Sometimes, she felt she was living a very bad movie and didn't know the lines or her role. So Sue Beth retreated, as she had as a child, to books, reading historical novels about what she thought was a "gentler time".

She glanced over at John with distaste as they drove to the party. She stared out at the dark, still angry about what had happened two days ago, when they had decided to visit the Civil War battlefield near Corydon. It had been a chilly day. They had had fun walking around the area. John, a collector of Confederate uniforms and guns, had been especially excited about the site. "We need to be here when they do a reenactment." She had agreed.

On the drive home on 62, she had been cold, and reached for the thermos.

"Would you like some tea?"

"Sure, sounds good." He had smiled.

She had twisted the cup off the thermos, pushed the mouthpiece up, and started pouring the hot tea. The smell of orange and spices filled the air, then the car bounced. The tea hit her left thigh and the car seat at the same time John's right hand slapped her upper leg.

Sue Beth turned to him startled and angry, ready to hit back.

He glared at her, and said in a steely voice, "Don't even think about touching me! I'll hit you so hard you won't be able to move!"

The anger oozed out of her. Sue Beth wanted to throw open the car door and run screaming from this marriage. Instead, she looked at her thigh with the bright red handprint. It hurt. She screwed the cup back on the thermos and put it on the floor. She lifted her purse, found the aloe bottle and rubbed some of the thick fluid on her thigh, then wiped the few drops off the car seat with a Kleenex.

She stared at John, who was glancing at her, his face softened, looking like a guilty little boy. Once that would have appeased her.

"Are you all right? I'm sorry."

"I need to use a bathroom."

"I'll stop at the next place I see."

Sue Beth didn't say anything. She watched the fields pass by.

Getting ready for the party this evening hadn't been fun either. She had been in the bathroom applying makeup at the mirror, and caught John watching her from the doorway, frowning. "What?" she grimaced.

"Are you wearing *that* to this *party? I want you to look really good, Sue Beth!"*

"I think I look good in this dress." She spread her hands across the material.

"You *don't.* Brown makes you look dowdy. *"*

She stared at him, feeling angry, but knowing better than to show it. He looked good in the dark green shirt, almost silky, with the charcoal slacks.

His thick, wavy, red hair so easily showed off his Scottish heritage.

"What do you want me to wear?"

He walked to the closet and pulled out a short, tight black dress he had bought her. *The slut dress.*

"I hate that."

"You look sexy in it. *Wear it. "*

Sue Beth stood in front of the long mirror as he zipped up the dress. He stared at her breasts pushing against the low cleavage and tweaked a nipple. "You'll be a hit at the party."

The Mercedes turned onto the winding narrow road that followed the softness of the hills. The mansion appeared at the top of one like some enormous square moon, lit inside and out.

"What a house!" John chortled. "One day, we'll live like this!"

She shook her head.

There were so many people inside the huge house with its numerous great rooms. The only feature she really noticed was the large fireplace with its wide stones, reminding her of streams and fish.

"Ma'am?"

She turned. A young man in dark slacks and a white jacket offered a tray of drinks.

"Yes, thanks."

She noticed his eyes make a quick survey of her body, before he walked away. Sue Beth took a sip of the wine. *Too strong.* She placed it on a nearby table decorated with platters of food. She picked up a canapé and tasted it. *Salmon and cream cheese.* Standing there eating it, she surveyed the room of people—not recognizing anyone. Every woman seemed to be in a black dress. We're all in our uniforms, she thought. *The Stepford wives.* John had disappeared as soon as they entered the home after meeting Lily Gaither, one of the hosts. She had seemed warm and sincere.

Voices and some easy listening music filled the room. Noises and smells—all kinds of colognes and foods—assailed her. She glanced at her watch. She knew John. They'd be there until the party ended.

At the far end of the room was a bar. Sue Beth walked slowly to it, feeling almost naked and afraid the dress might ride up. Men glanced her way and smiled; she smiled back. She knew the dyed blonde hair was an added attraction.

Taking the glass of ice and coke from the bartender, Sue Beth searched for John, and finally saw him oozing over a pencil-thin, black-haired woman in a brown dress. Sue Beth snorted. *Okay for her!* She watched as John stroked the woman's hair and whispered in her ear. She had seen her at other parties, and John had always ended up sniffing around her. He had even introduced her at one of them. What was her name? Vanilla? Rosemary? Some kind of spice. Cumin. She chuckled. Oh, yes, Pepper!

She backed against the fireplace stone and pretended she was part of it. It always worked—no one noticed her. She watched John glancing around. Ah, Pepper's husband had moved in—a sleek, black man who was quite gorgeous. Even though John looked her way, he didn't see her and walked to the bar.

Sue Beth walked to the large glass doors opened to the wide terrace. The view was amazing—the large lake at the bottom of the hill had party lights along the shore—the fog was rolling in.

"Nice view."

Sue Beth turned. A slender man with thinning hair stood near her. She smiled, "Yes, it is."

"Been here before?"

"No. You?"

"Yes, I'm Mark Gaither. I live here."

"Oh, well, of course, you would know the place well." She laughed nervously. *I'm babbling.*

"And who would you be?"

"Sorry, my manners seem to lift off at parties. I'm Sue Beth McDuff."

"John's wife?"

"Yes. How long have you lived here?"

"Let's see. Lily and I dreamed about a place like this for several years." He stared at the lake. "We created our own design and had it built about 15 years ago."

"It's quite interesting. Do you spend much time at the lake?"

"I do. I like to fish, and the lake has bluegill, perch, crappie, and some catfish. I take a small skiff out and fish at dusk or early morning. Actually, I don't catch much—I just like to be on the lake and think."

"You're lucky to have it. I think a lot when I'm driving back and forth to Corydon. I work up here several days a week."

He watched her, a slight smile on his lips. "What do you think about?"

She sighed. "Buffalo."

Mark chuckled. "Now I am surprised. That was not an answer I would have expected."

"What would you have expected?" Sue Beth liked him. She could feel herself relaxing with this older man who really seemed interested in what she had to say.

"I don't really know. Maybe a movie you had seen, books you read, something that happened at work, or things waiting to be done at home. Why buffalo?"

She told him about her fascination with the large animals.

"You know there's an old path across part of our land that the buffalo used a long time ago. The deer still use it, and I like to walk it."

"Really? Can you see the trail at night?"

"You wouldn't be able to see much. But if you'd like to go there, I'd be glad to show you."

When they returned up the walk to the house, Lily met them. "Where have you been, Mark? Oh, I didn't see you, Sue Beth!"

"I was showing her the buffalo trace, and we got to talking, and walking. I've been a lousy host and husband, I know. I'm sorry, Lily."

Lily grinned. "You!"

Sue Beth liked her smile and her easy manner with her husband. She wasn't mad at him! John would have been furious.

"I don't think you two realize it but it's quite late."

Mark glanced at his watch. "It's midnight! I am very sorry. Has everyone gone?"

"No. The Hudsons are still here, as usual. And your husband, of course, Sue Beth. He got very drunk!"

Sue Beth felt her face redden.

"I have him drinking coffee, hoping to sober him up a bit. He's better than he was."

It was 1:30 a.m. when they finally drove away, John at the wheel, insisting he was fine. Sue Beth was nervous. He erupted when they reached the two-lane road, his voice slurred, "So, where the hell did you disappear to? I didn't see you all evening."

"I saw you talking to that woman—Pepper. You looked like you were having a good time."

He stared at her a moment, then watched the road. "What's that mean?"

"I realized you're always around her at the parties. What's going on with you two?"

"I have to do something when I have a frigid wife."

Sue Beth just stared at him. "So you sleep with her?" She couldn't believe it.

"Of course, I do. What do you think? She likes having sex with me, unlike you. But what were you doing with Mark?"

She said wearily, "We walked around the lake. He showed me the old buffalo trail."

"And what else did you do?"

"We talked a lot. That was all."

He slapped her shoulder, and the car jerked. "Liar! You were gone for a long time. Lily couldn't find Mark, either. I wasn't that drunk. What happened?"

She cried. "Nothing happened. We just talked. He's a nice man. Nothing happened."

He muttered, "Yeah, sure."

The fog seemed to get thicker and thicker as they turned on the interstate. At first, John tried going the speed limit, but slowed quickly. "God, this is awful, I can barely see." He was silent for a while then spoke slowly, still slurring a bit, "How was Mark?"

"What do you mean?"

"Surely, he couldn't resist you in that dress."

"He was able to. We just talked about buffalo."

"God, Sue Beth, you think I'm that dumb and that drunk? Why would an older man like that who is known for having affairs all the time leave you alone?"

"I don't know, John. Maybe he respects you!" Sue Beth cringed.

Sarcasm had laced those comments.

John breathed deeply, and looked at her. "Where did he do it to you—against a tree or did he just lower you to the ground and lift your dress and shove it in?"

She could hear the anger building. Her hand clasped the door handle. They weren't going fast. If he tried anything again, she was jumping.

"You are a real bitch. TELL ME WHAT HAPPENED!"

Sue Beth noticed the forms in the fog before John did. Buffalo— so many of them—were standing on the road ahead! "John, look out!"

"Holy shit," he screamed, turning the car to the right. Just before it went off the road, Sue Beth opened the door and jumped. The car careened down the hill, the red lights fading.

Sue Beth hit the pavement, rolling like a bumpy cylinder, then stopped suddenly—her path blocked by one of the buffalo standing on the hill's edge. "Omphff!" She touched the thick hair, and felt safe.

Barely hearing the screams, glass breaking, and metal crunching, Sue Beth stood up, then leaned against the animal. The buffalo slowly backed off and butted her gently. She followed it through the fog into the hills on the other side of the interstate. The rest of the herd moved up next to her; she felt safe.

The fog and night dissolved; it was early morning. She looked up—enormous flocks of geese, sand hill cranes, whooping cranes and ducks flew over. They were so numerous they almost blackened the sky. Their calls crowded her ears and she smiled, content.

Officer Leroy Pinkerton, in his state police uniform, stood next to Clyde as the tow truck pulled out what was left of the car. The ambulance lights whirled in the thinning fog. Pinkerton said, "I'm surprised you didn't find the woman's body, too. It wasn't that far from your car!"

"I know. It was just so foggy."

The Constitution Elm

by

J. Baumgartle

Perhaps, on some day of gentle winds and sunny skies, we have met before. I am the spirit of the Constitution Elm. I capitalize my name because of the honorable service I was able to perform.

Men have ever been afflicted with extremes of weather, notably heat, which can cause weariness, irritation and slowness of mind. While their own buildings furnish shelter, of sorts—some shielding and darkness—they also confine the air. This leads to much pulling at collars and salt dampness of clothing. The skin chafes and the head throbs to distraction.

All this time, my branches are reaching through the breeze, holding myriads of leaves to be turned and refreshed from my deep roots. The men stumble from their confinement and find space to breathe in my shade. Their thoughts return. This is my fulfillment, my place among them.

You may consider that I no longer have branches; my roots are withered. Creosote embalms the remains of my trunk. All living things experience physical demise. Does this hinder the spirits of men? Do they not touch your memory and forest your past?

Wherever you find welcome shade, and rest in the whispered coolness of moving leaves, the collective beneficence of all trees sustains you, but especially that of the Constitution Elm.

Contributors

The Southern Indiana Writers Group has been more-or-less together since 1992. We began meeting monthly in a conference room in a local hospital. We now meet weekly to exchange information and expertise on everything from computers to poetry. The group also serves as a critique forum (in the same sense that a pack of wolves serves as food critics). Membership is limited, but visitors are welcome, and have been known to fit in so well they become members against their better judgment.

Bonnie Abraham After twenty-five plus years of writing letters disqualifying people from Unemployment Benefits, she retired in order to write something more pleasant. She writes short stories (many with Biblical themes), poetry and devotionals. Currently, she resides in Corydon with her mother's ghost.

Marian Allen lives in a big house in a little wood, which is not the only difference between Allen and Laura Ingels Wilder. She has published stories in print and on-line magazines, including Marion Zimmer Bradley's FANTASY Magazine, The Phone Book, PanGaia and Oceans of the Mind.

Jeannine Baumgartle writes poetry and fiction. Her work has appeared in publications such as *Green Meadow Press*, *Flying Island, Literally*, and Studio: *A Journal for Christians Writing* and won a residency for poetry at the Mary Anderson Center for the Arts . She and her husband live in the small town of Crandall.

Ginny Fleming considers herself to be foremost a screenwriter, as this is her favorite media. Because nobody thought to tell her she couldn't, after optioning 3 scripts for the unsold ensemble sitcom *"Tia"* (any producers reading this?), Fleming dived head-first into the shark-infested mulligan stew (How's that for mixing metaphors?) that is Hollywood scriptwriting. Her romantic comedy scripts can be previewed at *The Spec Script Library*, *Writer's Market*, and *Writers.Net*.

Fleming's take on hysterical fantasy (funny, that is), a novel she likes to call *Dragonsayver* (when she's not calling it Marvin), is a "Shrek-like" novel just begging to be made into an animated film (Fleming wonders if she should shove a tin cup in its hand and drop it on a busy intersection....). Besides her annual contribution to SIW anthology and a brief appearance in the Louisville Courier-Journal, Fleming is busy finding a home for *Keys of Illusion*, a Romantic/Suspense novel filled with magic, scuba, fantasy, a bunch of lavender stuff and little bit of sex. Multiple scripts are always in the works whenever Fleming manages to "channel" Jimmy Buffett, her "Muse" (Yeah, she knows Jimmy's not dead — Hopes for his continued good health, in fact — That just makes him easier to channel).

Joanna Foreman writes short fiction and slice-of-life vignettes. Her first collection of short stories, *Ghosts of Interstate 65,* was published in January, 2008. She is currently working on her first novel which is set along the River Walk in San Antonio, Texas. Her frequent weekend getaways to the River Walk keep her in touch with the imaginary characters living there. Above all, Joanna's first priority is family, although she occasionally experiences sudden urges to move to the moon for escape purposes. Her ten-year-old granddaughter advises her to take her cell phone so she can be kept abreast of the family's shenanigans while she is gone. Joanna and her husband Craig married barefooted on St. Augustine Beach in 2001. They built a modest home smack-dab in the middle of two wooded acres and will live happily ever after.

T Lee Harris is a writer and illustrator who has been a lover of mystery and the detective genre since discovering books. A graduate of Indiana University with a Bachelor of Fine Arts, T has been involved with radio production, game design, comic books and desktop publishing. Interests include participation in the Society for Creative Anachronism and Renaissance Faires, tailoring authentic costuming for re-enactors and playing online roleplaying games. Several novels are in progress featuring Sitehuti and Nefer-Djenou-Bastet, Josh Katzen and a series set in ninth century Ireland. Work has appeared in print and online venues including mystericale.com and Cat Tales.

Joy Kirchgessner lives in Corydon with her husband, Mike. Her interests are too vast to list on this page. She's a long time business woman of Corydon, and artist, whose nature paintings have been accepted into prestigious shows, photographer, whose photographs have joined her illustrations in our anthologies, equestrian, who enjoys trail rides, amateur archaeologist, who enjoys rock hunting and exploring new worlds—give her a chemistry set and a laboratory and she'd try to split atoms. Many years ago, Southern Indiana Writers tied her to a computer and wonderful stories blossomed from Kirchgessner's many interests. So now, she must add accomplished writer to that long, long list. She even has a novel or two in the early stages.

Glenda Mills resides in New Albany, Indiana with her husband and youngest son. She has a daughter and a son who no longer live at home and one grandchild. When she is not busy homemaking, homeschooling, attending soccer games, running the family taxi service, or volunteering at her church, she writes fiction, nonfiction, and poetry. She looks forward to the day when a person can actually be in two places at once.

Ardis Moonlight quite naturally is a fan of the moon and stars, and finally can see it all in Harrison County, a plus after 32 years in Louisville! A poet with poems published in several issues of "Calliope", an anthology published yearly by Women Who Write, she is also trying her imagination with short stories, and….gasp…considering a novel!

Teddi Robinson has taken several creative writing classes and has (With a lot of encouragement) just published her first book, *The Meddlers*. She is currently at work polishing the sequel for publication before the end of 2008.

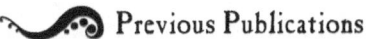 

Previous Publications by
Southern Indiana Writers

Indian Creek Anthology
Ghost Writers
Christmas Bizarre
Dragon: Our Tales
Grounds for Suspicion
2000 Tales
Way Out West
Unbridled Lust
There's Something Under the Bedtime Stories
Novel Ingredients
Write of Passage
Off the Rack
Beastly Tales
It's Always Something
Most Wanted

Visit our web site for excerpts of previous publications
and availability information:

http://southernindianawriters.com

www.ingramcontent.com/pod-product-compliance
Lightning Source LLC
Chambersburg PA
CBHW030527260626
47157CB00005B/1910

* 9 7 8 0 6 1 5 2 5 2 0 2 5 *